BEHIND
BARBED WIRE

ALSO BY DANIEL S. DAVIS

SPAIN'S CIVIL WAR
The Last Great Cause

MR. BLACK LABOR
The Story of A. Philip Randolph,
Father of the Civil Rights Movement

STRUGGLE FOR FREEDOM
A History of Black Americans

MARCUS GARVEY

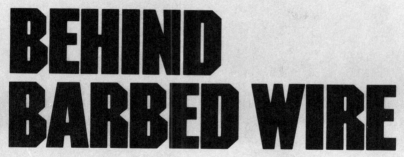

BEHIND BARBED WIRE

The Imprisonment of Japanese Americans
During World War II · by Daniel S. Davis

illustrated with photographs

E. P. Dutton · New York

The author and publisher gratefully acknowledge permission to reprint passages on pages 7, 103, 104, 110, and 112, from *Journey to Washington* by Senator Daniel K. Inouye with Lawrence Elliott. © 1967 by Prentice-Hall, Inc. Published by Prentice-Hall, Inc., Englewood Cliffs, N.J. 07632.

LIBRARY OF CONGRESS CATALOGING IN PUBLICATION DATA

Davis, Daniel S.   Behind barbed wire.
Bibliography: p.   Includes index.
Summary: Discusses the forced internment of Japanese Americans in camps following the attack on Pearl Harbor, their way of life there, and their eventual assimilation into society following the war.
1. Japanese Americans—Evacuation and relocation, 1942–1945—Juvenile literature. [1. Japanese Americans—Evacuation and relocation, 1942–1945. 2. World War, 1939–1945—Evacuation of civilians]   I. Title.
D769.8.A6D38   1981   940.54'72'73   81-3126
ISBN 0-525-26320-9   AACR2

Published in the United States by E. P. Dutton
2 Park Avenue, New York, N.Y. 10016

Editor: Ann Troy   Designer: Riki Levinson
Printed in the U.S.A.   10 9 8 7 6 5

CLEM ALBERS/NATIONAL ARCHIVES
Frontispiece: Barbed wire and armed guards replaced the freedom of civilian life for Japanese Americans during World War II.

for Michael

Contents

1   Day of Infamy   1

2   Pioneers and Prejudice   11

3   Decision   26

4   Countdown   41

5   Removal   56

6   Exile   67

7   Yes-Yes, No-No   83

8   "Go For Broke!"   98

9   The Courts   113

10   Going Home   124

11   The Road Back   141

    Selected Bibliography   156

    Index   158

1 Day of Infamy

The wind howled and huge waves slammed against the sides of the Japanese attack fleet. It was at anchor some 270 miles north of Pearl Harbor in the pitch black predawn darkness of the North Pacific.

On the deck of one aircraft carrier in the fleet, Commander Mitsuo Fuchida, air ace of the Imperial Navy, hoisted himself into a bomber's cockpit. He fastened to his flying helmet a white cloth headband that was the symbol of his readiness to die. Behind him on the deck, and on the five other carriers tossing nearby in the roiling seas, pilots climbed into 182 warplanes.

A green takeoff light flashed through the blackness. Fuchida's craft screamed off the runway and mounted skyward. The sounds of the sea, the wind, and the powerful thudding of propellers turning over were joined by the unison shouts of *"Banzai"* from the throats of thousands of sailors on the decks.

Plane after plane catapulted off the pitching carriers and climbed high above the gray cloud cover. Their destination: Hawaii. Their mission: to destroy the American fleet at Pearl Harbor and the American air force bases at Hickam and Wheeler airfields.

For almost two hours, the strike force of bombers, dive bombers, torpedo planes and Zero fighter escorts flew southwards. The sky slowly paled, first to a misty gray and then into a pale blue, pink-tinged Hawaiian daybreak. Shortly before 8 A.M. that fateful Sunday morning, December 7, 1941, the Japanese pilots approached the island of Oahu, sleeping in the Pacific, ten thousand feet below.

The light sound of church bells broke the early morning silence of the peaceful Hawaiian landscape. On board the ships of the American Pacific Fleet anchored at Pearl Harbor, sailors were sluggishly beginning their daily routine.

Then Commander Fuchida, in the lead, released a flare. It was a signal for the surprise attack that brought World War II to America. The fifty-one dive bombers climbed higher into the sky and then screamed downward. Seconds later, bombs were raining into the American fighter planes and heavy bombers parked wing to wing on the ground.

Smoke billowed up into the sky, and red flames licked the hangars and runways of the airfields. Two messages streaked across the Pacific. From Fuchida's command craft went the code words *tora, tora, tora*. This was a signal to the high command of the Japanese Imperial Navy that the surprise attack had begun. From the American base below him went the anguished radio message to Washington: "Air raid on Pearl Harbor—this is no drill."

The surprise attack on Pearl Harbor, December 7, 1941

Now it was the turn of the Japanese torpedo planes. Zooming in low over the water, they released their lethal torpedoes. They braked sharply upward to climb over the anchored ships in the harbor. Then each pilot looked back to watch the white foam of his torpedo's path. The blinding flash, earsplitting explosion, and jets of water spurting high in the air told him he'd scored a hit.

Most of the American ships were lined in pairs along the shore. They were sitting targets for the waves of dive bombers and torpedo planes that pummeled them. Sailors struggled across the decks to man machine guns and anti-aircraft guns. But they never had a chance to touch the attackers. Within minutes, the *Oklahoma* was rolling over

3

on her side while her crew scrambled overboard. The *West Virginia* listed heavily to one side, hit by half a dozen torpedoes. The *Arizona* was torn apart by a direct hit on her ammunition depot and sank. Over a thousand men were trapped in her flaming hulk.

The first wave lasted for half an hour and did most of the damage. Then the second attack wave pierced the smoke-filled skies to resume pounding the survivors. Now the Americans were able to put up a thick screen of heavy antiaircraft fire.

By about quarter to ten that morning, the last of the attacking planes, with their red ball insignia of the Land of the Rising Sun, had flown off to the vast emptiness of the North Pacific. There was no pursuit. There was no American chase to find their home fleet. America's air power was burning on bomb-pitted runways. Her much-vaunted Pacific Fleet was broken on the now still waters of Pearl Harbor.

It was time for counting losses. Of the eight battleships moored in the harbor, four were heavily damaged. The other four, along with three destroyers, were sunk. One hundred and eighty-eight planes were reduced to rubble. Another sixty-three were badly damaged. About 3,500 soldiers, sailors, and airmen were dead or wounded.

And it was only the beginning.

Within hours of the surprise attack on Pearl Harbor, Japan's forces struck across the South Pacific at Malaya, Thailand, Guam, Hong Kong, Singapore, the Philippine Islands, and at United States bases at Wake and Midway islands. The long cold war between America and Japan was finally broken. It was now a hot war, and in those dark December days, with the cream of her fighting force demolished, America was unsure of the outcome.

4

Smoke rises from Wheeler Airfield, where the Japanese raiders destroyed fighters and bombers in their hangars and on runways.

Every radio in the land blared reports of the terrible destruction at Pearl Harbor. Americans settled into a mood of shocked anger. All through that tragic Sunday, knots of people gathered at the gates of the White House. They watched tensely as diplomats and military men disappeared behind the iron fence of the president's mansion to draft plans for war.

War had been a long time coming. Europe was already at war—Hitler's Germany had been locked in combat with France and England for over two years. And the outlook for those two democracies was grim. On the other side of

5

the world, Hitler's ally, Japan, was to dominate Asia. Japan's military rulers had attacked China. They were engaged in a cold war of words with the United States, which demanded that Japan change her militaristic policies. Japan's answer was found in the bombs exploding on Pearl Harbor. This act stung even more since Japanese diplomats were negotiating in Washington, without even hinting that war was in the offing.

The next day, a grim President Franklin D. Roosevelt went to the House of Representatives to ask for a declaration of war against Japan. His words were destined to be remembered long afterward: "Yesterday, December 7, 1941—a date which will live in infamy—the United States of America was suddenly and deliberately attacked by naval and air forces of the Empire of Japan."

The coming of war released a powerful surge of patriotism in the nation. "Remember Pearl Harbor" became a rallying cry. Armed forces recruiting centers were swamped by young men anxious to fight. But there was also an explosion of hatred against Japan and all things Japanese. Four of the graceful Japanese cherry trees in Washington's Tidal Basin were chopped down by some misguided patriot. Much more serious was the spread of stories about supposed Japanese American spying and aid to the attacking pilots.

Americans knew that the coming days would be hard ones. They would be days bringing news of the death of loved ones. They would be days of shortages, rationing and worry. Perhaps they would even be days of more bombings, this time on mainland cities like Los Angeles and San Francisco.

But few Americans felt the oppressive weight of such thoughts more than the nearly 300,000 people of Japanese

6

descent who lived on Hawaii and on the mainland. Theirs was a special burden, for their ancestral homeland was now at war with the land they lived in.

For these Americans, the news of Pearl Harbor came as a horrible blow, met with shock and disbelief. The bombs that rained down upon the Pacific Fleet also sank their hopes of overcoming discrimination in America.

"Not only had our country been wantonly attacked," Senator Daniel Inouye, then a Hawaiian teenager, later recalled, "but our loyalty was certain to be called into question, for it took no great effort of imagination to see the hatred of many Americans for the enemy turned on us, who looked so much like him. And no matter how hard we worked to defeat him, there would always be those who would look at us and think—and some would say it aloud—'Dirty Jap.' "

Danny Inouye's immediate reaction to the attack was to leap onto his bicycle and pedal furiously to the first-aid station near Hickam Airfield. There he spent five days among the wreckage of the bombings, helping the doctors and nurses cope with the flood of suffering that so unexpectedly engulfed their hospital. As he picked his way among the clusters of stricken people clogging the Honolulu streets, an elderly Japanese man grabbed his handlebars and shrieked: "Who did it? Was it the Germans? It must have been the Germans."

Across an ocean and a continent, another Japanese American, Larry Tajiri, ducked his head in shame while making his way through the crowds in New York's Times Square that fateful Sunday night. "We are Americans by every right, birth, education and belief," he recalled thinking then, "but our faces are those of the enemy."

In California, where most Japanese Americans on the

mainland lived, disbelief gave way to stunned paralysis and, often, anger. Like other Americans, they gathered around radios or rushed out to buy special editions of the newspapers. The one-word headline "WAR" screeched from the front pages. Young Japanese Americans were defiantly furious. One high schooler shouted, "*They* are attacking *us*." Like their Caucasian friends and classmates, many made plans to join the armed forces.

Their elders, though, were fearful. Many huddled indoors, behind darkened windows, ashamed to face their white neighbors. The tug of old ties to their homeland and the strong ties to their children's land, America, created terrible conflicts.

Some sadly decided to part with mementos of Japan. They felt that clinging to their Japanese-language books and magazines and their family photos would be misunderstood by the American government. Frank Chuman's father took his family's ancient samurai swords, with their beautiful inlaid cases and exquisitely honed blades, to the backyard and buried them deep in the ground. Others burned their Buddhist family shrines, ceremonial dolls, and Japanese-style clothing.

They had good reason to be fearful. Hours after the attack on Pearl Harbor, FBI agents rounded up prominent members of the Japanese community. War talk had been in the air for months, and the government had the names of possible security risks. By evening, over 700 Japanese aliens had been arrested. Within four days, the number rose to 1,370.

People who had been leaders of community organizations or had connections with Japanese diplomats or trading companies were automatically regarded as dangerous and liable for arrest. Others, who may have contributed to

8

a cultural fund or been active in a community organization, were carefully watched for signs of disloyalty. The government also moved against German and Italian aliens to forestall spying or sabotage. These early arrests were made of suspicious *individuals*. While they were sometimes unfair, there was as yet no suggestion that all Japanese—or Germans or Italians—were disloyal.

The Japanese community immediately set out to convince their neighbors of their loyalty. The most prominent voice of native-born Japanese Americans was the Japanese American Citizens League. The league wired President Roosevelt: "We are ready and prepared to expend every effort to repel this invasion together with our fellow Americans."

JACL chapters launched war bond and Red Cross fund drives. They worked closely with the FBI and the armed forces to identify possible subversives within the Japanese community. Other organizations also rushed to declare their loyalty and to condemn the attacks on Pearl Harbor.

The friends of the Japanese Americans were quick to reassure them. Several California congressmen called for tolerance. Many Japanese Americans at school or on the job the morning after Pearl Harbor were reassured by Caucasian friends. These friends let them know that Americans who happened to be of Japanese descent would not be confused with the villains of Pearl Harbor. In some schools, principals called special assemblies to explain to the students that their fellow classmates were as much Americans as they were, and that all should pull together. The attorney general of the United States, Francis Biddle, promised: "At no time will the government engage in wholesale condemnation of any alien group."

And President Roosevelt, just one week after Pearl Harbor, told the nation: "We will not, under any threat, or in the face of any danger, surrender the guarantees of liberty our forefathers framed for us in the Bill of Rights. We hold with all the passion of our hearts and minds to the commitments of the human spirit."

Such words served to comfort the fears of many who recalled that throughout history, the passions of war have often unleashed ugly acts against defenseless minorities. But those words of reassurance, like the precious liberties they swore to preserve, would soon become subverted by American racism.

The Japanese Americans who were donating money to the war effort, who were volunteering for army service and defense jobs, who were burning their ties with their ancestral homeland, would soon be behind the barbed wire of American concentration camps.

2 Pioneers and Prejudice

The Japanese were latecomers to America. Their country was officially closed to the Western world until 1853, when Commodore Matthew C. Perry sailed his American warships into Edo Bay.

The first immigrants from Japan to settle in Hawaii came in 1868. Until the 1880s, only a handful settled in the United States. From then until 1924 when the United States excluded Japanese immigrants, less than 300,000 had settled in American territory. Japanese immigration was a trickle compared to the flood of immigration from Europe during the same period.

The typical Japanese immigrant was a young man from a farming family who had about eight years of schooling.

Japan was a mysterious island kingdom to most Americans when these first diplomats came to Washington in 1860.

12

He was not fleeing from oppression or extreme poverty, as most European immigrants were. Instead, he planned to return to Japan someday, to buy a farm or a business with savings from his years of work in America. He had strong ties to his family and to his native land, and was proud of his culture and its traditions.

The America he arrived in was raw and unformed. In many ways, California, where most Japanese immigrants settled, was still a frontier land. It had all the roughness and insecurity of a fast-changing society without traditions.

The Chinese had been the first Asian immigrants in the United States. Large numbers had come to build the railroads. But even as they contributed to the building of the West, they were victims of prejudice. Many were lynched or driven out of town by whites who feared economic competition. In 1882, western interests persuaded Congress to ban Chinese immigration.

It was into this hostile climate that the Japanese emigrants arrived. They closed their eyes to the prejudices of the Americans. They concentrated on working hard, getting ahead and saving their money.

Most of the newcomers were farmers, and it was to California's rich fields that they went in pursuit of their dreams. A typical new arrival became a migrant farm laborer. Many were hired as permanent laborers on large farms. But they were paid less than white workers.

After about five years, the new arrival would rent land of his own, often on a sharecropping basis in which the owner got a large portion of the crop as rent. Coming from the small, cramped, Japanese islands, the emigrant was struck by the vastness and richness of the California land. But his hunger for land was matched by the determination of the Americans not to allow him to own it.

Not all of the immigrants went into farming. Some became skilled loggers, miners, and railway workers. At one point, 13,000 Japanese were working on the railroads as section hands, laborers, and foremen. Other newcomers were important to the meat-packing, canning, and fishing industries. Still others found work as domestic servants, gardeners, housecleaners, window washers and cooks in the homes of white Californians.

Once they saved enough money, many immigrants who had decided to stay permanently opened businesses in cities. They usually preferred ports like Seattle or San Francisco, where ships from Japan docked, or towns near farms that employed Japanese workers. They opened boardinghouses, hotels, restaurants and small shops in neighborhoods called Little Tokyo. By 1909, the three western cities with the largest concentrations of Japanese—San Francisco, Los Angeles and Seattle—had over 500 Japanese-owned business establishments.

So long as the Japanese were few and confined to the hard, dirty jobs no one else wanted, they were tolerated. They had a reputation for being good workers. But, as the San Francisco *Chronicle* editorialized, "Japanese ambition is to progress beyond mere servility to the plane of the better class of American workmen and to own a home with him. The moment that this position is exercised, the Japanese ceases to be an ideal laborer."

This western anti-Orientalism was a regional version of the racism that gripped most Americans. The 1890s and early 1900s saw racist attitudes at their peak. Racial segregation was strong, and white superiority was a national belief. Anti-Japanese feeling became stronger with a surge in immigration—45,000 between 1903 and 1905. There were predictions of ultimate Asian domination of the

14

American West. A Stanford University sociologist told an anti-Japanese meeting that "it would be better for us to turn our guns on every vessel bringing Japanese to our shores rather than to permit them to land."

Racist stereotypes labeled the Japanese as "heathens" who could not become assimilated. Like other racial minorities, they were accused of being dirty, and their homes were called "nests . . . that pollute the communities like the running sores of leprosy." People believed them to be "sneaky," "untrustworthy," and "degenerate."

They were suspected of disloyalty, too. In the early 1900s, newspapers and films fastened on what was called The Yellow Peril and spread fantasies about a Japanese invasion of the United States and Mexico.

Fear of economic competition was behind much of the hostility toward the Japanese. The immigrants were willing to work harder for less money and for longer hours than native workers. Unions did not see the solution to the problem in higher pay and better working conditions for the Japanese, but in excluding them from jobs white men wanted.

The opening of a Japanese store often led to picketing, rock throwing, and appeals for white boycotts. When the Japanese entered the laundry business, for example, white workers organized the Anti-Jap Laundry League.

Joining union members in anti-Japanese agitation were farmers, patriotic organizations such as the American Legion, and anti-immigration groups formed to agitate for Oriental exclusion. Politicians were among the most enthusiastic backers of the "Keep California White" line. Anti-Asian incidents multiplied during election years as candidates would whip up racist feelings to win votes.

The anti-Japanese movement led to friction between the

15

U.S. and Japan. After the San Francisco earthquake in 1906, mobs attacking Asians led to official protests by the Japanese consul.

That fall, the city's school board ordered all Japanese children to attend a segregated school. The order was front page news in Japan, which protested to President Theodore Roosevelt. He wrote, "The infernal fools in California . . . insult the Japanese recklessly, and in the event of war it will be the Nation as a whole that will pay the consequences."

Roosevelt managed to get the order canceled, and in 1908 negotiated the Gentlemen's Agreement with Japan, limiting immigration. Only Japanese who had homes in America and their wives, parents and children would be allowed to enter. Until the Gentlemen's Agreement, immigrants were usually unmarried men. After the agreement, women made up the bulk of immigrants.

While some men returned to Japan to marry and brought their wives back with them, many more arranged marriages through the mails. This was not as unusual as it may seem today, for arranged marriages were traditional in Japan, as in many other countries.

The new brides joined their husbands behind store counters and in the fields. As their children grew, whole families worked together. This was an important factor on Japanese-run farms. The farms were often small plots of substandard land that could be made to yield harvests only by intensive hand labor.

As the farmers prospered, they became targets of politicians and agricultural interests. Hoping for documentation that would win support for restrictions on the Japanese, they backed a study of Japanese farmers. Contrary to what was expected, the 1910 report declared:

"The Japanese landowners are of the best class. They

are steady and industrious, and from their earnings purchase land of low value and poor quality. The care lavished upon this land is remarkable, and frequently its acreage value has increased several hundred percent in a year's time. Most of the proprietors indicate an intention to make the section in which they have located a permanent home, and adopt American customs and manners.''

In short, model Americans. The report, though, was rejected, and a major effort was launched to get the Japanese off the land.

Over the objections of President Wilson, who, like Roosevelt, feared trouble with Japan, California passed several alien land laws. The Issei—Japanese citizens residing in the United States—were forbidden to buy land, and their leases on rented land were limited.

The Issei soon found ways to get around the law. They bought land in the names of their children, who, born in America, were citizens. Others bought land through corporations they set up, which were nominally headed by whites.

These laws were a terrible blow to the Japanese, even though they found ways to evade them. "When those laws were passed, it hurt here," said one Japanese woman, her hand on her heart. "We had no power. We had nothing."

California's lawmakers did not mention the Japanese in these land laws. Instead, the laws were directed at "aliens ineligible to citizenship," a group limited to the Issei.

America's original naturalization law was passed in 1790, long before Asians came to her shores. It limited citizenship to "free white persons." Later amendments provided rights for Africans and other Asians to acquire citizenship. But, with some exceptions, the Japanese immigrants were denied the right to become American citizens.

Japanese immigrants faced racism and discrimination. Signs like this one were common in Hollywood in the 1920s.

The same device was used by Congress to cut off immigration from Japan in the National Origins Act of 1924. This law limited immigration, especially from southern and eastern Europe. But it also barred immigration from countries whose people were "ineligible to citizenship," again affecting only the Japanese. Enforcement was not strict, so some immigration took place, but never at the previous pace.

Despite persistent discrimination, the Japanese were making important contributions to America. By their hard work, they helped to transform California into a richer, better place than they found it.

The Japanese farmers made dead land come to life. One

18

Family members worked together to make truck farms yield fruit and vegetables, which were sold in nearby cities.

Japanese immigrant transformed wasteland in the Sacramento Valley into rich rice-producing farmland through pioneering techniques. Another, George Shima, drained swamplands and created a potato farming empire that employed 500 people and brought him a fortune. He won the nickname The Potato King. Others took land white farmers had given up on and made it produce berries and other fruits, and even vineyards.

Since they had less money and smaller farms than other California growers, the Japanese concentrated on the truck-farming industry, selling their produce in nearby cities. The result was lower prices and fresher food for city dwellers on the West Coast.

By 1941, Japanese farmers were producing much of California's vegetables. Over a third of the total income from commercial truck crops in the state came from small Japanese-operated farms. Their average size was less than a fifth of the size of other farms and amounted to only 2.7 percent of the state's croplands. From this farming base, Japanese businessmen expanded to operate large-scale fruit combines, as well as retail fruit stands and grocery stores—over 1,000 in Los Angeles alone.

By the eve of Pearl Harbor, the Japanese community had grown from the bare handful of the late 1800s to 127,000 people in the continental United States. Three-fourths of them lived in California, where they accounted for only about 1.5 percent of the state's population. The vast majority were now Nisei—native-born American citizens whose parents were Japanese.

The Japanese community was marked by its peculiar immigration patterns—almost exclusively young men in the beginning, then younger women, and relatively few small children until the 1920s. Thus, by 1941, the typical family consisted of Issei parents—the father in his late fifties or early sixties, the mother in her late forties—and Nisei children in their late teens or early twenties. And there were many unmarried elderly men—the result of fewer Japanese women due to immigration restrictions.

The group which traditionally provided leadership—men in their thirties and forties—was small in comparison to other age groups of Japanese Americans. While the Issei were dying off or reaching retirement age, the Nisei were still too young to provide leadership. This generation gap was accompanied by a cultural gap common to immigrant groups and their children.

Since they were cut off from the larger society by dis-

20

crimination and by language difficulties, the Issei built their own community organizations. There they re-created the special traditions and qualities of Japanese life. Japanese associations were found wherever Japanese lived. Originally formed to protect the immigrants from discriminatory attacks, they had become social clubs that aided the poor and the sick. But they also sent donations to Japanese soldiers fighting in China, increasing American suspicions of Issei disloyalty.

Most Issei also belonged to *kenjinkai*, associations of people from the same *ken*, or locality. The *kenjinkai* became an important factor in the immigrants' progress in America. Members often helped find jobs for each other and pooled savings to help finance new businesses.

There were also church organizations, both Christian and Buddhist, Japanese language schools, and a host of other groups. Just about every person belonged to one, and many joined several. The social highlight would be the annual picnic, featuring games and competitions for the younger people and homemade feasts for all. More ominous to their white neighbors was the annual celebration of the emperor's birthday. This featured elaborate ceremonies that included bowing before his picture and singing Japanese patriotic songs.

It was natural for the Issei to remain loyal subjects of their emperor. After all, their adopted country refused them citizenship. So if they renounced their ties to Japan, they would be people without a country. Besides, the Issei had no desire to deny a heritage of which they were fiercely proud.

But the Issei also followed the traditional Japanese code of loyalty to the place where one lives. So they were as loyal to the United States as were members of other foreign-born groups. The Nisei, however, considered themselves Americans whose parents happened to come from Japan, just as their classmates' ancestors happened to come from England, Germany or Russia.

The Issei were strict parents. Smoking, dancing, parties and dating were either forbidden or strictly supervised. They were critical of the Nisei's adoption of American ways. Communication between parents and children was made especially difficult by the language problem. Many Issei spoke English poorly, while few Nisei mastered Japanese, despite attending language schools.

Many parents demanded that their children follow old-country customs such as bowing to their elders. They insisted on traditional values of obedience to authority, conformity to the community standards, and fulfillment of the duties one owed to parents and to the community. The family was a solid unit, with the parents, especially the father, in full command. A disobedient child would be kept in line, not with a spanking but by being told that he was bringing shame on the family by his actions.

Japanese cultural traits were viewed with suspicion by native Americans. Their natural reserve and understatement led to their being called inscrutable. And their lack of American-style openness resulted in the "sneaky" label. Prejudiced people stigmatized the tightly organized Japanese community as "clannish." They interpreted the ties to Japan as "disloyalty." Thus, the Japanese suffered from racist stereotyping although, as a group, they were more law abiding, harder working, and more studious than the general population.

Since the Nisei were in contact with the white world more often than the Issei were, they felt pressures to succeed and to prove their Americanism. Urged on by their parents, who felt education would lead to better opportunities and to acceptance by the white world, the Nisei studied hard. They often won the best grades at school, and were more likely to complete high school and college than other groups.

But the Nisei found that many companies refused to hire them or would accept them only in low-level jobs. College graduates often found they couldn't even obtain interviews for white-collar jobs.

For a Nisei to be admitted to a medical school or to get an engineering job was almost unheard of. So educated Nisei were often forced to accept low-paying and sometimes menial occupations. Some joked that a beautifully stacked fruit display indicated the clerk was a trained engineer.

Thus, the Nisei were caught between two worlds: that of their parents, which they largely rejected as too "Japanesey," and that of their fellow Americans, who rejected them.

By the late 1930s, with Japan at war with China and in a cold war with the United States, foreign policy debates disrupted Japanese American households. The Issei, who read only Japanese newspapers, were convinced Japan was in the right. They took pride in Japan's rise as a world power. After a lifetime of defeats and discrimination, they were finally rooting for a home team that was winning.

The Issei found it hard to accept Nisei arguments against Japan's aggression. They were upset when the Nisei took part in anti-Japan demonstrations and picketed against the sale of war materials to Japan. The Nisei, like other Americans, were alarmed by Japan's militarism and that of her allies, Nazi Germany and Fascist Italy. In part, they also felt a need to exhibit their Americanism at a time of anti-Japanese feeling.

To protect their own interests and to combat discrimination against the Issei, the Nisei formed the Japanese American Citizens League. The JACL limited membership to American citizens, and thus was an almost exclusively Nisei group. It was formed from the merger of similar local groups in 1930. It quickly won some notable victories.

The JACL helped win federal laws granting citizenship to Issei veterans of World War I and enabling Nisei women to marry Issei without losing their American citizenship. It waged local campaigns to desegregate swimming pools and movie theatres. It lobbied against the laws designed to squeeze the Issei off the land and out of the fishing industry.

More such laws were being considered in the tense atmosphere of the late 1930s. Rumors spread that Japanese fishermen in California were really officers of the emperor's navy. Japanese farmers were rumored to be planning to poison wells and to sabotage military bases in case of war.

A national magazine stated there were 250,000 Japanese "soldiers" in California. *Life* magazine headlined an article: "The Nisei—California Casts an Anxious Eye Upon the Japanese Americans in Its Midst."

By mid-1941, relations between the United States and Japan had become so bad that economic relations were broken and alien assets frozen. This meant the Issei could not touch their U.S. bank accounts. Nisei had to bring their birth certificates to banks to prove they were citizens and thus not subject to the freeze. Many Issei, cut off from their funds, could not pay their workers and their bills, and some stores failed because of the action.

The Nisei tried to convince Americans they were as loyal as any other group of citizens. A major goal of the JACL was to educate the younger generation to the principles of Americanism. It began to work actively with armed-forces

24

intelligence units and with the FBI. Its flag-waving loyalty seemed at times to be imbued with super-Americanism. In 1940 it had adopted the JACL creed, in which each member extolled America's virtues, made no mention of her persistent racism, and pledged to "assume my duties and obligations as a citizen, cheerfully and without any reservations whatsoever, in the hope that I may become a better American in a greater America."

These sentiments helped to win some support for the Nisei. But too many people still agreed with an American Legion leader who declared in 1939, "In case of war, the first thing I would do would be to intern every one of them."

Thus, when war did come, the American nation had to decide how it would treat the Japanese in its midst. Should America accept their declarations of loyalty? Should she put them behind barbed wire fences? The decision would tell Americans more about themselves than it would about their Japanese minority.

3 Decision

In late 1941, the bulk of America's Pacific Fleet was a charred hulk amid the ruins of Pearl Harbor, and the Japanese Army was sweeping almost unopposed through Southeast Asia. A massive invasion of the United States seemed possible.

In that highly charged atmosphere, Californians were convinced they were the next target of attack. Many people believed—and spread—the most outlandish rumors. Many accepted Secretary of the Navy Frank Knox's mistaken claim that there had been widespread sabotage at Pearl Harbor. In January 1942, an official commission investigating the attack reported—without evidence—that Japanese spies had aided the enemy. One popular tale said that Japanese farmers on Hawaii planted their crops in the shape of arrows pointing to Pearl Harbor to guide the attacking planes.

None of this was true. No evidence has ever been uncovered that any sabotage had taken place in Hawaii. The only persons ever accused of spying during the war were of American or European origin. Apart from Japanese diplomats, no Japanese resident in the United States was ever accused of aiding Japan's war effort.

And Japan was never capable of invading the West Coast. In the months following Pearl Harbor, there were some instances of Japanese military action near the coast. A few American ships were attacked by submarines; and in February 1942, oil tanks in southern California were shelled in a hit-and-run attack from the sea. Throughout this period—and for the rest of the war—the Japanese Fleet was 5,000 miles away from the continental United States.

But panic ruled civilians and military men alike. On December 8, 1941, the army reported Japanese bombers near San Francisco, and the next day, thirty-four battleships off the California coast. Then it reported the main Japanese fleet just 200 miles from San Francisco, and followed that with a wild report of an impending attack on Los Angeles.

Part of the steady flow of false reports was due to incompetent radio operators. They kept picking up radio stations in Japan and reporting the broadcasts as secret messages from spies to warships lying off the coast. Federal authorities called in to investigate the radio operations reported the situation as "pathetic to say the least."

Another reason for the army's constant attack alerts was the nervousness of staff officers. The complete surprise of Pearl Harbor made them prefer pushing panic buttons to being blamed for another disaster.

Lieutenant General John L. De Witt was in charge of defense
of the western United States after the attack on Pearl Harbor.

The Western Defense Command was responsible for the
defense of eight states—Washington, Oregon, California,
Arizona, Nevada, Utah, Idaho and Montana. Its chief was
Lieutenant General John L. De Witt, an excitable veteran
officer. His staff described him, in the days after Pearl
Harbor, as having "gone crazy."

De Witt was especially concerned about the enemy

aliens in his command area, particularly the Issei. Like many people, he saw little difference between the Issei and the Nisei, American-born citizens. For De Witt, as he later told a congressional committee "A Jap's a Jap. They are a dangerous element. . . . There is no way to determine their loyalty. . . . It makes no difference whether he is an American; theoretically he is still a Japanese, and you can't change him . . . by giving him a piece of paper."

De Witt blew hot and cold on the internal security issue. One day he would give assurances that there was little threat of espionage or sabotage. The next he would be screaming for the removal of all enemy aliens from his command.

De Witt and the army were responsible for the military defense of the West. The Justice Department, which included the FBI, was responsible for internal security, and for keeping watch on enemy aliens. Enemy aliens are residents who are citizens of a country with whom the United States is at war. Thus, they are subject to governmental actions that do not apply to citizens of the United States.

The officials closest to the problem—in the FBI, army and navy intelligence services—were satisfied that no internal security threat existed. The few individuals who were suspected of disloyalty could be easily dealt with. In fact, FBI raids immediately following Pearl Harbor had rounded up just about everyone on the list of suspicious aliens.

De Witt's superiors at the War Department wanted to take over the Justice Department's role in the West Coast's internal security. They thought the civilians at the Justice Department were too soft and too concerned with civil liberties. They wanted increased military control and stricter measures. They also wanted to increase their own powers at the expense of the civilian authorities.

The provost marshal general of the army, Major General

Allen W. Gullion, pushed for greater army control of the security situation. He sent his aide Major (soon to be Colonel) Karl R. Bendetsen to San Francisco as the liaison between De Witt and the Justice Department. Bendetsen encouraged De Witt to demand stricter control of the aliens.

Early in January 1942, the Justice Department caved in to military pressure and agreed to stricter controls on enemy aliens. This included spot raids on their homes.

Soon, FBI agents raided homes of Japanese residents. They peppered them with questions about their loyalty and searched for forbidden items.

The raids sparked a new wave of fear in the Japanese community. People who had kept mementos of the old country now followed the lead of those who had destroyed them just after Pearl Harbor. Many Issei wives packed traveling bags for their husbands, so that if the FBI took them away in the dead of night, they would have a fresh change of clothes and toilet articles with them.

Hundreds of FBI agents trundled out of Japanese neighborhoods loaded down with cartons of contraband—items enemy aliens were forbidden to have in their possession. These included cameras; knives, including Boy Scout hunting knives; and explosives sometimes used by farmers. The results of these raids could easily have been predicted. Attorney General Biddle reported to the president:

"We have not uncovered through these searches any dangerous persons that we could not otherwise know about. We have not found . . . any evidence that any [dynamite or gunpowder] was to be used in bombs . . . nor have we found any gun in any circumstances indicating that it was to be used in a manner helpful to our enemies. We have not found a camera which we have reason to believe was for use in espionage."

30

In other words, the mass investigations, raids and seizure of property turned up no suspicious evidence at all.

But General De Witt said that the failure to discover evidence of sabotage preparations only proved "that such action will be taken." Thus the Japanese were in a no-win situation. Their homes were raided because they were suspected of disloyalty. Then, when no evidence was found, it was said they were planning sabotage in the future.

About all the raids achieved was to deepen the insecurity of the Japanese. They were painfully aware that their neighbors were suspicious of them. Many Californians asked: If the Japanese are so innocent, why is the FBI raiding their homes?

The Japanese community was concerned about what other actions might be taken against them. Rumors spread—rumors of FBI brutality, of beatings by Filipinos in revenge for Japan's invasion of the Philippine Islands, and of lynchings in rural areas. One Nisei recalled that "cars of Caucasian kids used to drive around the Japanese section yelling names at us and we didn't have any comeback. There was always the fear that some mob demonstration would take place. At one time a wild rumor went around that a mob was coming to burn the whole Japanese town down. Other people claimed that they had received threatening notices over the phone."

The next blow fell on January 29, 1942. The attorney general, at the request of the War Department, prohibited enemy aliens from living in the San Francisco waterfront area or near the Los Angeles airport. That meant Japanese, German and Italian citizens living in those zones would have to move. Within the next ten days, some 133 additional areas were prohibited. Most of them were around airports, dams, power plants and other places where sabotage was feared.

De Witt had been clamoring for such action. But it had taken him almost a full month to come up with the specific areas from which he wanted aliens barred. Then he kept adding new zones, to the dismay of the Justice Department, which had to enforce the restrictions. On February 4, the coastline from Oregon to the Los Angeles suburbs was made a restricted area. Enemy aliens were subject to a strict curfew. They had to be in their homes between 9 P.M. and 6 A.M. During the day, they could be only at their homes, at work, or in places within five miles of their homes.

De Witt kept adding even more prohibited zones. The frustrated attorney general wrote Secretary of War Henry L. Stimson that the new requests meant evacuating thousands of people. He said the Justice Department "is not physically equipped to carry out any mass evacuation. It would mean only the War Department has the equipment and personnel to manage the task."

This may have been the military's strategy all along— to increase their demands on the Justice Department until it would give up and turn the whole matter over to the generals.

This power struggle was going on behind the scenes. As far as the public was concerned, enemy aliens, and especially the Japanese, appeared to be a threat to security. Anti-Japanese racist feelings, always strong, now were in full swing.

Newspapers and magazines regularly used the term *Japs* in headlines and stories. The racial slur was used both for enemy soldiers and for Nisei. Stories informed readers how to tell the difference between Chinese and "Japs." One columnist urged his readers "to be careful to differentiate between races. The Chinese and Koreans both hate the Japs

32

more than we do. . . . Be sure of nationality before you are rude to anybody.''

Columnists and radio commentators charged that Japanese Americans were disloyal and urged their removal from the West Coast. The popular columnist Henry McLemore, wrote: "I am for immediate removal of every Japanese on the West Coast to a point deep in the interior. . . . Herd 'em up, pack 'em off and give them the inside room in the Badlands. Let 'em be pinched, hurt, hungry and dead up against it. . . . Let us have no patience with the enemy or with anyone whose veins carry his blood.''

Thus the news media popularized racism and blurred the important differences among the enemy, the peaceful and loyal Issei, and the native-born American citizens—the Nisei.

Business interests also urged removal of the Japanese, often hoping to get rid of Japanese competitors or to steal land belonging to the Japanese. Such businesses and farmland were estimated at a value of $140 million in California alone. Racism and greed came together as one farm leader frankly admitted:

"We're charged with wanting to get rid of the Japs for selfish reasons. We might as well be honest. We do. . . . If all the Japs were removed tomorrow, we'd never miss them in two weeks, because the white farmers can take over and produce everything the Jap grows. And we don't want them back when the war ends, either.''

The press, important business and farm interests, and the traditionally anti-Oriental patriotic organizations all were calling for removal of the Japanese. Western congressmen now switched from pleas of toleration to strident calls for removal of the Japanese. They received support from openly racist southern legislators. One southern sen-

Japanese American children join their classmates in the pledge
to the flag.

ator declared: "They are cowardly and immoral. They are
different from Americans in every conceivable way, and
no Japanese . . . should have a right to claim American
citizenship."

California's governor, other state officials and mayors
also urged removal of the Japanese. The state's attorney
general, Earl Warren, warned that: "Unless something is
done it may bring about a repetition of Pearl Harbor."
Warren later became chief justice of the U.S. Supreme
Court and was known as a fighter for civil rights. But in
early 1942 he was planning to run for governor and followed the traditional California political ploy of riding the
"Japanese menace" to higher office.

Earl Warren was one of many California politicians who claimed the Japanese American residents threatened U.S. safety.

Warren differed from the typical Japanese-baiters by insisting on strict legality. When the state fired its Japanese American employees, Warren condemned the act as unconstitutional racial discrimination. But he looked to the military for action that state and civil authorities could not take. The Constitution protected citizens such as the Nisei. But Warren thought the Japanese were a threat. And if civil authorities could not legally remove them, then "The Army that is charged with the security of this combat zone has the right to do it."

Attorney General Biddle still insisted that "American citizens of Japanese origin could not . . . be singled out of any areas and evacuated with other Japanese," because they had constitutional rights that had to be respected. Some military men also opposed evacuation. General Mark Clark, assigned to study the problem, decided that removal from strategic areas, FBI scrutiny and spot raids could deal with potential sabotage. Military intelligence experts said that no special security threats were posed by the West Coast Japanese. They warned against wasting scarce military manpower in an evacuation program.

But a handful of War Department officials pressed relentlessly for the removal of the Japanese. The key figure was General Gullion, the provost marshal. His office would be the key to evacuation. He had influence with top Army and War Department officials. His aide Colonel Bendetsen was now chief strategist in the operation. He drafted endless memorandums and proposals to keep the issue alive and to influence policymakers. Bendetsen guided General De Witt, making sure he backed total evacuation. He swung the changeable general back in line when he went through one of his regular retreats from that hard-line position.

Their civilian superiors, Secretary of War Stimson and his assistant secretary, John J. McCloy, did not oppose the views of the military commanders. The army was responsible for the safety of the West Coast, and its views were shared by powerful congressmen. Legal and constitutional safeguards had to take a backseat to security measures. As McCloy told Biddle during one heated exchange, "If it's a question of the safety of the country [and] the Constitution . . . why, the Constitution is just a scrap of paper to me."

The War Department prepared a memorandum for President Roosevelt, outlining possible actions. These ranged from limited restricted zones around defense installations to complete removal of all Japanese, citizens as well as aliens. On February 11, Stimson called the president to get his instructions and was told to "go ahead and do anything you think necessary." But, Roosevelt added, "be as reasonable as you can."

With the green light from the White House, events now moved swiftly. All the haggling and negotiating with other federal agencies could end. De Witt was instructed to prepare a final set of recommendations. Bendetsen was at his side to make sure it would include a provision for removal of all Japanese.

Opposition from the Justice Department crumbled. Biddle was still concerned about civil rights of citizens. But he was not willing to oppose his president and the senior member of the Cabinet, the respected Henry Stimson. Lawyers from both the Justice and War Departments worked on a final draft of a presidential order that would give the War Department control over the Japanese.

Alarmed by the mounting calls for removal, the Nisei, led by the JACL, tried harder to convince the public of their loyalty. Petitions were signed and meetings held, all pledging support for the war effort. The Nisei pleaded with their fellow Americans to act fairly and to judge them as individuals, not as part of an enemy group. At one such meeting, on February 19, a Nisei speaker expressed confidence that America would act fairly, and that "our greatest friend is a man who is the greatest living man today— President Franklin Delano Roosevelt."

But his confidence was misplaced. That very evening, the president signed Executive Order No. 9066, sealing the fate of America's Japanese.

The order authorized the secretary of war "to prescribe military areas . . . from which any or all persons may be

President Franklin Delano Roosevelt betrayed the hopes of the Nisei by signing Executive Order No. 9066.

excluded, and . . . the right of any persons to enter, remain in, or leave shall be subject to whatever restrictions'' the military chose to impose. The order also gave the War Department authority to remove people from such areas, house and feed them ''until other arrangements are made,'' and to take any steps necessary to ''enforce compliance with the restrictions.''

38

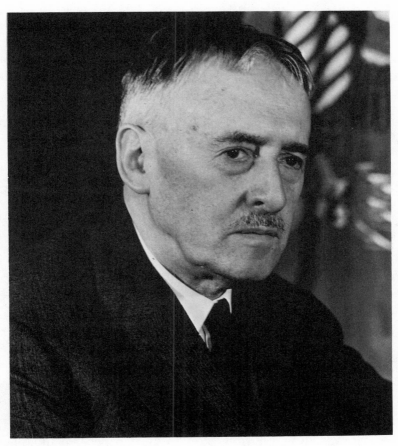

Executive Order No. 9066 gave Secretary of War Henry L. Stimson authority to enforce evacuation orders against Japanese Americans.

Such sweeping powers had never before been granted to the military outside areas where actual fighting was going on. Under the order, the military had the right to expel citizens from their homes. It went far beyond the restrictions placed on enemy aliens in December, January, and early February. No limits were set on the size of the "prescribed areas."

The legal basis for the order was the Constitution's grant of war powers to the president. But Congress was asked to pass a law enforcing the order by making its violation a federal crime. Government lawyers wanted to add a further touch of legality to what many thought was an unconstitutional violation of civil rights. In March, almost without serious debate, Congress passed Public Law 503. It has been called "more of a military order than a law." Senator Robert A. Taft called it "the sloppiest criminal law I have ever read or seen anywhere."

Although the Japanese were not mentioned once in the nearly 1,000-word executive order, everyone understood it was directed against them. The War Department immediately ordered De Witt to designate restricted zones from which he was to exclude all Japanese. It suggested that "in the most critical areas you may consider it necessary to bring about an almost immediate evacuation." Although De Witt was ordered to exclude the Japanese, he was told he should act against only those aliens from Germany and Italy whom he considered serious security risks. Thus, European enemy aliens were given more consideration than Japanese Americans who were citizens.

The order was a terrible blow to the Japanese. Although many feared the worst, the JACL cautioned: "Do not become overly alarmed or panicky at this news. . . . Let us hope for the best and be prepared to cooperate with the government in this near-martial law step. . . . This rule is to apply to all nationalities. . . . It is not a matter of discrimination as much as it is a matter of military expediency. The final test is, of course, in its application."

And that test was soon to come.

4 Countdown

The Japanese were now in limbo. They had no way of knowing if they'd be forced to move from their homes and if the Nisei, as citizens, would be treated differently from the Issei.

Into this confused atmosphere, the Tolan Committee entered to take testimony about the "Japanese problem" in several West Coast cities. Headed by Representative John H. Tolan of California, the committee was made up of members of both branches of Congress. The Nisei welcomed the hearings, hoping to convince Congress, the government and the public that a policy of racial exclusion was wrong.

Mike Masaoka, national secretary of the JACL, testified that the Japanese were prepared to make any sacrifices to help the war effort, even evacuation. But he demanded that their rights as citizens be protected from "political or other pressure groups who want us to leave merely from motives of self-interest."

The Nisei leaders felt they had to agree to military judgments that might lead to their evacuation in order to demonstrate their loyalty. Other Japanese Americans called this a sellout. They insisted that there were no real military reasons for their removal. And the Issei were scornful of the Nisei's attempts to save themselves on the grounds of citizenship. Even if such arguments worked, they would still leave the Issei, as noncitizens, subject to evacuation.

The committee heard other witnesses who supported the Japanese Americans. These included labor leaders and a civil rights lawyer who pointed out that "treating persons because they are members of a race constitutes illegal discrimination, which is forbidden by the Fourteenth Amendment whether we are at war or peace."

But such voices were rare. The majority of witnesses called for removal of the Japanese. Some tried to ensure that no actions would be taken against German and Italian aliens. One witness stressed the likely damage to national morale if the parents of baseball hero Joe DiMaggio, Italian aliens, were forced to move from their home near San Francisco's waterfront.

The star of the hearings was California state Attorney General Earl Warren, who insisted that "there is more potential danger among the group of Japanese who are born in this country than from the alien Japanese who were born in Japan." Warren came equipped with a long list of strategic places in southern California where, he said, "Japs" lived. He neglected to point out that their farms were near oil wells, highways and factories because they were the only farmers willing to work on such small, poorly located plots. And he trotted out the old argument that because no sabotage had been committed, it "is because it has been timed for a different date. . . . We are approaching an invisible deadline."

The committee hearings accomplished nothing more than a public airing of the issue and a chance for at least a few pro-Japanese voices to be heard among the din of demands for their removal.

During the hearings, there were events that illustrate the fears then infecting West Coast citizens.

On February 23, a Japanese submarine surfaced off the coast of Santa Barbara and fired on the mainland. It caused no serious damage but raised fears of further enemy actions.

The next night came the "Battle of Los Angeles." Radar screens picked up an object headed toward the city from the Pacific Ocean. A total blackout was called, and antiaircraft guns pumped 1,400 shells into the night air. Twenty Japanese were arrested for supposedly signaling the invaders. The next day, with the city in a panic, the army claimed up to five unidentified planes had tried to penetrate its air defenses. But the navy said there were no planes at all—a weather balloon had drifted loose, setting off what an official called "jittery nerves."

If these incidents demonstrate the tense atmosphere in those days, the removal of the Japanese residents from Terminal Island showed how Americans proposed to deal with their fears.

Some 500 Japanese families lived on Terminal Island, near a U.S. Navy base at San Pedro. Most of them were headed by fishermen. In late January 1942, the island was marked by authorities as a "strategic area" from which enemy aliens would be barred. A few days later, FBI agents invaded the island. They arrested 336 Issei the government considered potentially dangerous, and shipped them to detention camps in Montana and South Dakota. On February 25, the remaining Japanese on the island, most of them now women, children and elderly men, were ordered to leave.

Within hours, Terminal Island became a scene of desperation and havoc. The confused Japanese packed what little they could with the help of volunteers. Secondhand dealers descended on the island to buy up furniture, family heirlooms and other items for a fraction of their value. Some Japanese, in tears, broke their treasured possessions rather than let such vultures steal them away. With the help of the JACL, they were temporarily resettled on the mainland.

Soon, the experience of the Terminal Islanders would be shared by all the Japanese in the coastal states. On March 2, De Witt announced that enemy aliens and all Japanese, whether citizens or not, had to leave Military Area Number One, a strip running the length of the West Coast and extending into southern Arizona. The ban on other enemy aliens was never enforced, but the Japanese were urged to leave.

Although De Witt was planning to eventually remove all Japanese from his eight-state command, they were told to move from Military Area Number One to other parts of the region. Military Area Number Two was made up of the remaining parts of Washington, Oregon, California and Arizona. The Japanese were promised they could resettle there and "in all probability not again be disturbed."

To help supervise the movement of civilians out of the coastal strip, De Witt set up the Wartime Civil Control Administration (WCCA). It was under the command of Colonel Bendetsen, the chief architect of the evacuation program. The WCCA began to build two "reception centers"—at Manzanar, California, and Parker, Arizona—to temporarily house up to 20,000 people. These would serve as "resting points from which the Japanese . . . could proceed further eastward once they had secured jobs and community acceptance."

This was a cruel deception, for the army made no attempt to prepare the public outside Military Area Number One to receive the refugees. About 4,000 people moved into areas just east of the prohibited coastal region, and about as many moved further east. But they were met with hostility. Armed men patrolled highways at the California-Nevada border to turn back Japanese families. Main streets sported No Japs Wanted signs. The governor of Kansas ordered his highway police to stop Japanese trying to enter the state. Most people decided that if the Japanese were considered dangerous in San Francisco, they would be just as dangerous in Wyoming or Colorado.

The voluntary movement of the Japanese out of the barred areas was turning into a shambles. The military empire-builders were still out to convert the operation to a more ambitious scale. General Gullion proposed a chain of internment camps run by the army. But Secretary Stimson and top army officers were dead set against pulling 35,000 troops out of combat in order to guard those camps. They convinced the president to create a civilian agency to handle evacuation problems.

On March 18, Roosevelt established the War Relocation Authority. The WRA was to plan for the orderly evacuation of the expelled Japanese and provide "for their relocation, maintenance and supervision." Milton Eisenhower, brother of General Dwight D. Eisenhower, was named to head the new agency.

Milton Eisenhower quickly established a small staff and prepared to cope with a situation that was getting out of hand. Government policies demanded exclusion of the Japanese from the coast. Voluntary individual resettlement into the interior was a flop. Now the WRA had to come up with a solution acceptable to the army, as well as to the public.

Eisenhower proposed that the Japanese be resettled in small work camps scattered across the country, with jobs in the surrounding neighborhoods or on government projects. But public resistance killed that plan. Governors from western states refused to accept any Japanese not under armed guard. So the government had no choice but to plan for large guarded camps with little or no contact with the surrounding population.

With the failure of the policy of voluntary evacuation, the army devised a plan for forced removal. Just a few weeks after being officially encouraged to move out of Military Area Number One, the Japanese still there were forbidden to *leave* it. All Japanese, aliens and citizens alike, were instructed to stay put until the army came to move them out.

De Witt issued Civilian Exclusion Orders, removing the Japanese. The first of these orders, on March 24, applied to Bainbridge Island. Several hundred Japanese lived there, across Puget Sound from the large Seattle naval yard. Gun-slinging soldiers in full battle dress swooped down on the island to post the order. It gave the Japanese only six days to pack and be ready to move. On March 30 they were herded aboard a ferry to the mainland. Then a train took them to an assembly center at the Puyallup fairgrounds in Washington.

The exclusion of the Bainbridge Islanders was a rehearsal for the mass removal of the West Coast Japanese. The smooth efficiency of that operation led to similar orders for each of the 108 areas the army decided would be emptied of Japanese.

Each of the areas was home to roughly 1,000 Japanese, and in each the WCCA set up a Civil Control Center to handle the operation. Exclusion usually came in the form of an order posted on walls, telephone poles and buildings, printed in newspapers, and announced on the radio. Signed by De Witt, the orders were addressed "To All Persons of Japanese Ancestry." They instructed that "All Japanese persons, both alien and nonalien" would be evacuated in a week's time.

No exceptions were made. Japanese who were citizens were included, and were further insulted by the term *non-aliens*. No provision was made for Japanese married to non-Japanese or their children. The sweeping definition of *Japanese* included anyone with a Japanese ancestor. This affected even individuals who had no apparent Japanese features or who no longer had ties to the Japanese community. Thus, the army's exclusion of the Japanese was as sweeping a racial law as any put forth by the Nazis with whom we were at war.

The order instructed each family head or individual living alone to report to the Civil Control Center, usually a storefront or a school. There they got detailed instructions on the evacuation and tags for identification and baggage. They filled out forms and were assigned a number. The center also helped arrange for storage of property and the sale or lease of homes, livestock and other major items.

On Evacuation Day (E-Day), the Japanese were instructed to take with them only what could be carried by an individual or family. They were restricted to clothing,

This confused little girl is surrounded by her family's belongings as she waits for the bus to an assembly center.

bedding, linens, kitchen utensils, and personal effects. Whatever could not be fitted into the allowable luggage had to be left behind or stored by the government "at the sole risk of the owner." Many Japanese who had carefully crated and packed refrigerators, furniture, and other goods never saw them again.

The Japanese were frightened, uncertain of what might happen to them, and fearful of being turned loose in wilderness camps. Many fell prey to scavengers offering to buy up cars, furniture and homes at prices a fraction of

48

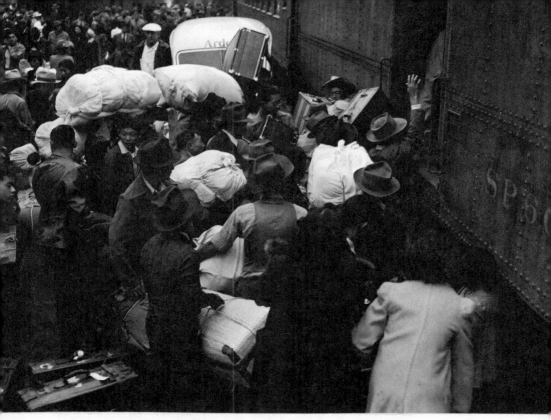

Evacuees clamber aboard a train bound for the Manzanar Assembly Center, bringing the few belongings they were allowed to take with them.

their true value. Often, Caucasian friends offered to let their Japanese neighbors store goods with them, and to look after property left behind.

In one town after another, from the Canadian border south to Mexico, the West Coast was stripped of its Japanese. E-Day saw knots of confused older Issei gently led aboard buses by their children. Their grandchildren, not understanding the tumult about them, laughed and cried or stared quietly, fingering the large white identification badges pinned to their jackets.

Japanese-owned stores in Los Angeles were sealed and pad-
locked as their owners were moved to assembly centers in the
spring of 1942.

CLEM ALBERS/NATIONAL ARCHIVES
Assembly centers were hastily put up to house the evacuees.
This one was at Santa Anita racetrack.

Meanwhile, the army was feverishly building temporary
centers to house the refugees its orders created. Fairgrounds, racetracks, parks, and other large, unused spaces
became scenes of hurried construction work by army engineers. In only 28 days, they threw up temporary housing
for over 100,000 people.

All but three of the sixteen centers, innocently called assembly centers, were in California. The largest was at the
Santa Anita racetrack, which became a temporary home to
over 18,000 men, women and children. Each of the centers
was circled by barbed wire fences patrolled by armed military police. Watchtowers manned by soldiers with rifles
loomed above.

At Manzanar, as at other centers, the civilian evacuees were guarded by armed soldiers in full battle dress.

Military police in watchtowers guard the camp at Santa Anita.

The West Coast Japanese were imprisoned by military power and treated much like prisoners of war. Alone among the alien nationals of the countries with whom we were at war, the Issei were singled out for special treatment. No other citizens were dragged from their homes and placed under lock and key because of their ancestry, as were the Nisei.

By June 2 the Japanese were in assembly centers, almost all of them wracked by feelings of confusion and disbelief. As one young Nisei wrote before leaving his home:

"You never thought such a thing could happen to you, but it has. And you feel all tangled up inside because you do not quite see the logic of having to surrender freedom in a country that you sincerely feel is fighting for freedom."

For the Nisei especially, the discovery that their citizenship was held valueless by white Americans was terribly painful. But by and large their leadership was determined to make the best of a bad situation. A JACL leader condemned the motives of those who were behind the expulsion of the Japanese. But he went on to say, "We are going into exile as our duty to our country because the president and the military commander of this area have deemed it a necessity. We are gladly cooperating because this is one way of showing that our protestations of loyalty are sincere."

Many Nisei and their elders, however, condemned the JACL as a collaborator. They denied that such sacrifices were necessary to prove loyalty to a nation that wasn't willing to listen to proof and was racist in its treatment of the Japanese.

The JACL leadership had thought of ways to stop the evacuation. But government officials told them that the

Japanese would be forced to leave the West Coast at the point of bayonets if necessary. They decided that resistance would only lead to bloodshed. Compliance might at least demonstrate loyalty. At best, it might enable the Japanese themselves to have a greater voice in determining where they would go and how they would live. It was a painful choice, and the Nisei leadership's decision not to fight a lost cause divided and embittered their shattered community.

No other decision was possible for them because public opinion, the military, and the elected leadership stood together in dislike and mistrust of the Japanese.

Elsewhere in the country, people were simply indifferent. To an Iowa farmer, a Chicago factory worker, or a Boston businessman, we were at war with Japan. If the president, the military, and the people of the region in which most Japanese Americans resided thought they were disloyal, well, that settled the matter. At the end of March, a public opinion poll found that 93 percent of Americans believed evacuation of alien Japanese was "the right thing." And 59 percent approved the removal from the West Coast of Japanese Americans who were citizens. Almost two-thirds of those polled thought the evacuees should be kept "under strict guard as prisoners of war."

Other countries, too, went on the rampage against their own Japanese. Canada enacted similar removal and internment programs that swept her west coast of resident Japanese and locked them away for the duration of the war. Many Latin American countries were shaken by anti-Japanese riots. Some shipped their Japanese people to the United States at the urging of Washington. They were held in the camps our government set up. The idea was to use them as hostages in dealing with the Japanese government. Ironically, after the war ended, the U.S. government tried to deport these Latin American Japanese on the grounds that they had entered the country without passports or official visas.

Even stranger was the treatment accorded Hawaii's large Japanese population. If any region had the right to be sensitive about the dangers of Japanese in a war zone, it should have been the territory of Hawaii. It was the site of Pearl Harbor, the gateway to the Pacific and the staging area for America's war against Japan. But while the mainland Japanese were herded into camps, no such action was taken against Hawaii's far larger Japanese population. Why?

It wasn't for lack of trying. Immediately after Pearl Harbor, instructions were given for Japanese in Hawaii to be watched carefully, and the navy insisted on removal of all Japanese to protect against sabotage. Plans were made to either deport the Japanese to the mainland, ship them to one of Hawaii's smaller islands, or place them in concentration camps on Oahu, the largest island.

But reason prevailed. Hawaii's Japanese numbered some 160,000 people: over a third of the territory's population. They were essential to its economy, since they worked in the skilled trades like construction, which were important for the islands' defense. There were not nearly enough ships to transport 160,000 people over 2,400 miles of ocean to the mainland, nor were there enough soldiers to guard them.

So Hawaii's Japanese were spared the brutal treatment given the West Coast Japanese. Their sheer numbers saved them—you cannot mistreat over a third of the population the way you can a tiny minority. Less than 2,000 Japanese Hawaiians, identified as possibly dangerous or sympathetic to Japan, were moved to mainland camps; but the rest survived in relatively normal conditions. They were harassed and regarded with suspicion, but they managed to escape the fate that awaited the Japanese of the West Coast.

5 Removal

E-Day brought relief from the months of suspense and fear for the Japanese, but it also brought the bitter shock of cold reality. Many of the Issei held to traditional Japanese attitudes of obedience to authority and acceptance of fate. Thus, they resigned themselves to leaving their homes and neighborhoods for the dim uncertainties of internment. But for the Nisei, American citizens brought up to believe in the fairness of their country and their democratic rights, evacuation was a nightmare come true.

Names became numbers—Monica Sone remembers the way each person in her family had to wear a lapel tag, not with his or her name, but with #10710. At ten in the morning, the Sones stood with hundreds of other Japanese, surrounded by tagged luggage waiting for the buses that would sweep them into a new life. When the vehicles arrived, so too did armed soldiers, rifles at the ready, watching silently as the Japanese boarded. A news photographer rushed into a bus, pulled an embarrassed family out, and snapped their picture. It appeared the next day with the caption: "Japs good-natured about evacuation."

Similar scenes were repeated elsewhere on the coast. Miyuki Hirano remembers boarding a truck and hearing shouts of "Jap, go home." Others remember sitting in fear while a soldier boarded the bus with his bayonet unsheathed. Many recall the hostile faces of people leaning out of nearby apartment windows and the cold grimness of policemen and guards. But they also remember the kindness of other whites who brought water and food for the evacuees as they waited for the buses to arrive. In a gesture of protest, one evacuee showed up in his U.S. Navy uniform bearing decorations he had won in World War I.

Some never boarded the buses. Hideo Murata, an Issei who was a veteran of U.S. Army service in the First World War couldn't believe the government he had fought for could do this. When E-Day was announced, he asked his friend, the sheriff, if it wasn't a practical joke or some awful mistake. But no, it was no joke. He would have to go to a camp. Instead, he went to a local hotel, paid in advance for his room, and killed himself. When the authorities found his lifeless body, they saw, clutched in his hand, the Certificate of Honorary Citizenship presented to him the previous Fourth of July by Monterey County as "testimony of heartfelt gratitude, of honor and respect for your loyal and splendid service to the country. . . ."

The buses, trucks and trains headed for the temporary camps, called assembly centers. There the Japanese were to be held until permanent camps were ready. The army built and controlled the assembly centers. But the permanent camps would be under the jurisdiction of the War Relocation Authority, the civilian agency that would come to control every aspect of the Japanese's lives.

Most of the centers were bleak, uninviting places. As Monica Sone's bus traveled through the countryside, people commented on the large number of chicken houses. Then the bus turned, entered a wire-fenced gate, and deposited its riders in front of the "chicken houses." They were to be the temporary homes at the Puyallup Assembly Center.

Jeanne Wakatsuki remembers the bus carrying her family and neighbors being pelted by what they thought was a heavy rain. But it wasn't. It was a windswept dust and sand storm, typical of the violent weather of California's Owens Valley, site of the Manzanar camp.

As the vehicles entered the camps, the people fell silent, numbed with shock. They realized they would be forced to stay behind those barbed wires, in those shacks, in that awful climate, for who knew how long.

Many of the centers were not ready to receive the thousands of evacuees they'd have to hold. Army engineers built the centers, but evacuee volunteers helped to finish them. They helped make them livable and organized some semblance of normal life within them. Hospitals and schools had to be set up, and mess halls established. Without the cooperation of the evacuees, chaos would have resulted. Even with their cooperation, fear and confusion were rampant.

Many of the evacuees spent their first days in shock, unable to adjust to the primitive living conditions, the prison atmosphere, and the lack of privacy. The housing facilities stunned the new arrivals. "When I first entered our room, I became sick to my stomach," wrote one man from the Tanforan Center. "There were seven beds in the

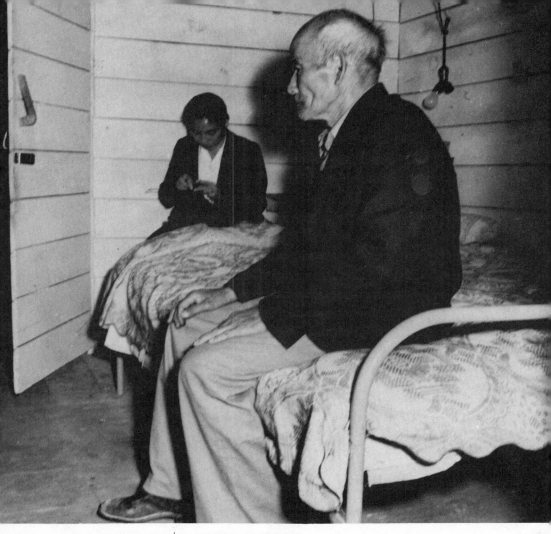

Small, bare rooms shocked the evacuees.

room and no furniture nor any partitions to separate the males and the females of the family. I just sat on the bed, staring at the bare walls.''

Families were housed together, although in Manzanar, one-room apartments were shared by two families. The authorities planned in terms of the nuclear family—mother, father, children. But the Japanese family was an extended

DOROTHEA LANGE / NATIONAL ARCHIVES
At Tanforan, many evacuees had to live in remodeled horse stalls.

family that included grandparents, uncles, aunts and cousins. Many were outraged at being separated from family members who lived in other parts of the camps. Single people shared barracks, and no one had privacy. Even where barracks had been partitioned into apartments, there was an open space between the top of the partitions and the roof. This allowed noise to waft across the length of a building. Bachelor quarters at the racetrack at Tanforan consisted of a huge barracks under the grandstand without adequate light or air. It had one entrance for 200 men.

Thousands of people were housed in former horse stalls at converted racetracks. Only four days separated the removal of horses from the arrival of people at Santa Anita.

60

The pungent smells of the animals resisted the straw and disinfectant that were supposed to make the stalls fit for humans. At Puyallup, former pigpens were turned into apartments.

Toilet and shower facilities were even more shocking, especially to the fastidious elderly Issei. In many camps, toilets were "one big row of seats, that is, one straight board with holes cut out about a foot apart with no partitions at all and all the toilets flush[ed] together." Some people erected partitions out of cardboard, then out of scrap lumber. More than thirty years later, Betty Kozasa was still upset: "The degradation of it all, having to go to shower with 150 people at one time and no shower curtains . . . these are the things that rankle and stay with me."

Food was another problem, especially in the early days when kitchen sanitary conditions were bad and hot water was unavailable for washing dishes. Long lines snaked around the mess halls. When the evacuees finally reached the serving counters, they faced unappetizing mess kits filled with sausages, slabs of white bread, pasty rice and dessert, all running together. This was exactly the opposite of the traditional Japanese manner of serving and arranging food to please the eye.

Called assembly centers, the camps were actually prisons. No one could leave them. Wire and concrete fences surrounded them. Armed sentries patrolled. Floodlights from watchtowers played along the grounds at night. Regular inspections were made, and each family had to be indoors after dark. "When they have roll calls, the sirens ring," wrote one evacuee. "I get so scared that I sometimes scream. . . . I run home as fast as I can and then we wait about five minutes and then the inspector comes to check and see that we are all at home."

Meals were taken army style, in mess halls.

Friends were allowed to visit, but permission had to be applied for in advance. At first, visitors could talk with evacuees only through the wire fences under the watchful eyes of armed guards. Later, reception halls were built. But visits were still made under prison conditions. At Santa Anita, the visiting room was divided by a long table. Inmates had to stay on their side of the barrier, forbidden to shake hands. But even this was better than being in camps that were isolated and thus received few visitors.

Within these prison camps, some attempts were made to introduce democratic self-government. At Santa Anita, a constitution was drawn up by the inmates. All camps had self-governing councils with representatives from each block.

The evacuees saw the need for a representative body to negotiate with the camp officials and to prevent excesses by army troops.

But real governing power was lodged in the authority, as was made clear by its heavy-handed censorship. Except for Bibles and dictionaries, all Japanese-language literature was banned. Newspapers were heavily censored. The editors of the Manzanar *Free Press,* a camp newspaper, agreed that the only thing free about the paper was its subscription fee.

There was much to do in the running of the centers. They were like small towns. There were schools, health clinics, mess halls and other basic services that had to be staffed by the inmates. Some of the centers grew their own food, so there was a call for farm workers. And in the larger ones, factories were set up. Since no family got more than $7.50 per month as an allowance, it was necessary for people to work to buy clothes and necessities not provided by the administration.

But the pay scales for workers were set very low. Administrators feared a public outcry if the Japanese were to make more money than soldiers drafted in the army. So center workers were paid according to skills—$8 a month for unskilled laborers, $12 a month for skilled workers, and a high of $16 a month for such professionals as doctors and dentists. Many professionals worked alongside white civilian employees, often less qualified, who were paid far more.

But paid work at such low pay scales did not prevent hardship. The head of one family that had three members working wrote: "The small salary we get from the jobs is not sufficient for my cigarettes or for my daughter's necessities; the ready cash we carried from Los Angeles is getting low every day. If Peace will be restored in some future, I won't have any money left in my possession; this Problem worries me days and nights, but I don't have any idea for solution."

The center inmates worked as cooks, servers, porters, and dishwashers in the community mess halls. Others worked in maintenance, as gardeners, janitors, drivers, mechanics and in similar jobs. Many worked in schools, recreation facilities, and medical services. There were secretaries, clerks, typists, messengers, and center police.

At the larger centers, such as Santa Anita and Manzanar, factories manufactured camouflage nets. Because making the nets was considered war work, only citizens— that is, Nisei—could be employed. Many Issei were angry at what they considered unfair discrimination. Nisei workers also complained of poor conditions in the factories, low pay, and unfair production quotas. Strike talk flourished, but the factories turned out nets by the thousands and helped the U.S. war effort.

The most valued jobs were those that took people out of the centers in what were called work release programs. The war created a manpower shortage, and it looked like crops would rot in the fields. Farmers now pleaded with the government to send them Japanese workers to harvest the crops.

Beginning in the fall of 1942, thousands of center inmates were released temporarily, to serve as contract farm laborers. They were paid at the same rate other farm workers got—more than the center pay scales. They were sent to Oregon, Utah, Idaho, Wyoming and Montana to harvest sugar beets, potatoes and peas. A Utah newspaper editorialized: "If it had not been for Japanese labor, much of the best crop in Utah and Idaho would have had to be plowed up." California, though, refused to allow the Jap-

A factory for making camouflage nets was one of the work projects at the Manzanar center.

anese to work on the farms. The federal government imported 30,000 Mexican workers to help harvest California's crops.

For the Japanese, the work release program was more than a way to earn some badly needed money. One sugar beet worker wrote of his experience that "I can't make much money, but the idea of being a 'free' man and eating the things you like—the way you like them—is mighty fine." But they feared an incident that might trigger anti-Japanese violence or threaten the work program. So the workers kept pretty much to themselves. They stayed out of restaurants and bowling alleys and other places where danger lurked.

Temporary release was also given to young people to attend college. Helped by prominent citizens, government agencies, Quakers, and others, Japanese student committees worked to get students into colleges. It wasn't easy. Some major universities flatly refused to accept any Japanese students. Others wanted FBI clearance for each student as an entrance requirement. But eventually enough colleges proved willing to accept Japanese students. About 4,300 left the assembly centers and internment camps for schools in the East and the Midwest.

The War Relocation Authority, the agency responsible for the Japanese, favored such programs. The WRA wanted to move people out of the centers and into a more normal civilian setting. But public opinion was still largely against such a move. People argued that the evacuation of the West Coast Japanese was in itself proof of guilt.

So instead of moving people out of the assembly centers, the WRA eventually moved them into permanent camps. The WRA tried to make it easier for evacuees to leave the camps and relocate in other parts of the country. But the WRA's main task was to manage the concentration camps, an ugly term officials were forbidden to use. As its first director, Milton Eisenhower wrote President Roosevelt in his letter of resignation in June 1942, "a genuinely satisfactory relocation of the evacuees into American life" would only be possible after the war, "when the prevailing attitudes of increasing bitterness have been replaced by tolerance and understanding."

As 1942 drew to a close, return to civilian life seemed far away for the 120,000 Japanese caught in a system that held them as helpless pawns.

66

6 Exile

Throughout the summer of 1942, trains and buses crammed with Japanese Americans crossed the Sierra Nevada to deposit their unwilling passengers in permanent camps for the duration of the war.

There were ten such camps in all. Among them, only Poston, in Parker, Arizona, and Manzanar had been assembly centers. The others were specially built and placed under the control of the War Relocation Authority. Two were in California—Manzanar and Tule Lake. Two were in Arizona—Poston and Gila. The others included Heart Mountain, in Wyoming; Minidoka, in Idaho; Topaz, in Utah; and Granada, in Colorado. The two camps farthest from the West Coast, Rohwer and Jerome, were in Arkansas.

Set in rural areas and in the less populated states, these camps soon became among the largest towns in their vicinity. Poston grew to hold over 18,000 people. Even the smallest of the camps, Granada, with its 7,600 residents, was a sizable town in Colorado.

By the beginning of November, 119,803 people were living in these concentration camps. The WRA was naturally very sensitive about what the camps were called. They named them "wartime communities." The prisoners were "residents" or "colonists." But the reality of armed guards, barbed wire, and lack of freedom led even President Roosevelt to privately refer to them as concentration camps.

All of the camps were hurriedly built to standard plans for basic army camps designed to last only a few years and to house soldiers without families.

Almost all of them were in desolate areas, whipped by severe weather conditions. A WRA official described Minidoka as "hot, dusty . . . nothing growing but sagebrush, not a tree in sight." The average summertime temperature there was 110 degrees. Monica Sone recalled that "the sun beat down from above and caught us on the chin from below, bouncing off the hard-baked earth, and browning us to such a fine slow turn that I felt like a walking southern fried chicken."

Poston was even hotter, and one evacuee wrote that "we spray water in the rooms and wet our cots and we carry wet towels over the head whenever we go out." Heatstroke was a constant danger there, as at Gila and other camps. Dust storms added to the misery. At Manzanar and Topaz, they seared the skin with hot sand particles. When it rained, the sand cover turned to mud.

Tule Lake was not a lake at all, but was built on sandy

Most camps were in isolated, windswept locations. Manzanar and others were ripped by dust storms.

land that had once been a lake bottom. The summers were dry and not extremely hot. But the cold, long winters sent temperatures to well below zero. The two Arkansas camps—Rohwer and Jerome—were in damp swampy lowlands that had some of the most dangerous poisonous snakes on the continent.

It was in such places that the government dumped its Japanese population in the summer of 1942. These permanent camps were not completed when the trains and buses brought the evacuees to the sunbaked dust bowls that were to be their new homes.

They arrived at camps studded with half-built barracks,

TOM PARKER/NATIONAL ARCHIVES
The swampy Jerome, Arkansas, camp suffered heavy rainstorms.

and with bulldozers still tearing at the earth. The newcomers were brought to the mess halls where they were given water and salt tablets. Next they lined up at long tables where WRA employees filled out forms and took their fingerprints. Then they were sent off to another building to collect housing assignments and to take a quick physical exam. From there, it was onto trucks that dropped them at the barracks.

70

Evacuees used scrap materials to help make their quarters livable.

Then it was time to create some sort of home out of the 20- by 25-foot room each family was allotted, time to take their assigned supply of straw and fill their assigned sacks to make mattresses. Each person was given an army cot. Other than that, the rooms were bare, without closets, chairs, shelves, or any other furniture.

The first weeks were occupied by trying to make homes out of barracks. People salvaged scrap lumber with which to build furniture. They made curtains, rugs and other items that might make the bleak rooms more homelike. They investigated their new surroundings. Then came the business of creating a community.

The WRA decided that the evacuees should govern themselves through elected community councils, with representatives from each block. But this attempt at democracy fooled no one, since the councils had no real powers. They could only advise the camp officials. Everyone over the age of eighteen could vote for the council. But only citizens—the Nisei—could hold office. This increased the Issei's bitterness and drove new rifts between them and the Nisei.

The Nisei-only rule meant that most council members were young people. At Tule Lake, the average age of the council members was about thirty, while most Issei were over fifty. "Where in this world," asked one Tulean, "was there a city, or even a little village, run entirely by young people aged thirty and under, without men and women of maturer years participating in its affairs?" The policy was changed in 1943, but by then the damage was done.

The councils were meant to act as channels of communication between the inmates and the authority. They were also to adopt and enforce local laws, just like any other town council. Within months, most of the camps had elected councils and set up groups to design community constitutions.

Private business was barred, but a system of cooperatives was quickly established. All sorts of small stores—groceries, repair shops, beauty parlors, and others—were set up. Each camp had its own newspaper. Slowly, the camps came to resemble small towns, except for the grotesque presence of armed guards and barbed wire.

Each camp quickly established a school system. In Poston alone, there were 175 teachers. Even so, classes were very large. One first-grade class had 78 children under 1 teacher with no assistants. Many of the teachers were young

Nisei education-school graduates. Others were Caucasians under contract to the WRA. Before the camp finally closed, Poston would have 70 school buildings.

It was WRA policy to provide jobs for everyone who wanted to work. Many found employment in the various administrative offices, in the mess halls and laundries, and in other camp activities. It was understood that the evacuees would perform work needed to make the community more livable. But they refused to do things they considered the authority's responsibility, such as constructing pipelines or other basic facilities. While some plunged into work to help forget the past, others were content to, as they often put it, "take a vacation."

Older Issei, veterans of years of hard farm labor, spent their days playing the Japanese checker game, *go,* playing cards, and carving wood. Poetry groups flourished. Thousands registered for adult education courses in camps that offered them. Drama groups staged plays, both Western style and traditional Japanese *Kabuki* dramas and *Bunraku* puppet shows. The Japanese transformed many of the barren campsites with delicate wood sculptures and finely crafted cactus and rock gardens.

Such activities helped make life in the overcrowded camps a bit easier, a bit more natural. It helped many of the evacuees to overcome the climate, the sense of imprisonment, and the disruption of family life. Before the war, the typical Japanese family had been very close-knit. But under camp conditions, children were freer of parental control. Teenagers roamed in bands without the former tight parental supervision. Even minor domestic decisions involved dozens of neighbors who shared the barracks, and sometimes included block managers and community councils.

As time passed, life behind the barbed wires took on aspects of normalcy. Camp residents threw themselves into a variety of activities, including the traditional Japanese game of *go*.

Camp residents staged elaborately costumed plays based on old legends, and undertook artful landscape projects.

For the younger camp residents, there were basketball games on homemade courts.

Authority in the camps was wielded by the administrative staff, all employees of the WRA. Although they worked closely with evacuee representatives, when their day's work was ended, they were free to go. They lived in homes outside the camps or in government-built and -furnished houses within them. As a teacher at Poston observed, "We had too much and they didn't have enough."

This in itself would have stirred resentment. But WRA workers also had to go through inmates' mail and packages. They had to confiscate such innocent items as cameras, which were forbidden. Some were inexperienced or just plain incompetent, while others were prejudiced. It was clear to everyone that their superior status was due primarily to their being white. Racial antagonism between the staff and the evacuees was often present. It was made worse by the policy in some camps of not allowing WRA staff to become too friendly with the Japanese.

There was also tension between the generations. The Issei resented their near total dependence on their native-born children, even for such simple tasks as filling out registration cards. Some Nisei, now freed from tight traditional family controls, lorded it over the Issei.

Some Issei taunted the Nisei with the fact that their citizenship could not keep them from the camps. The more energetic Issei set up planning boards that gradually took over real power from the Nisei-dominated community councils. Diehards among them were convinced that a Japanese victory in the war would free them and restore their homes and farms. The frustrations of years of racist victimization combined with fears for the future and made many Issei resentful and angry.

For the two-thirds of the evacuees who were Nisei and American citizens, every day in the camps provided fresh evidence that their loyalty and patriotism were scorned. Even the army rejected them, classifying Japanese Americans 4-C in the draft. This was a category reserved for enemy aliens, not for native-born citizens.

One Nisei expressed his confusion this way: "Japan doesn't want us and this country doesn't want us either. . . . Even if I want to be a good American, they think I'm supposed to act like a Jap and they don't want to give me a chance. They think I am inferior. That's why I want Japan to win this war in a way. Then in other ways I want America to win. I don't know. I just don't give a damn."

But some Nisei plunged into camp work. They tried to make life a bit easier for their elders. They studied and worked so they'd be ready to pick up new careers when the war ended. And they responded eagerly when opportunities were finally granted to join the armed forces or to leave the camps for jobs on the outside.

Perhaps the most alienated of all were the Kibei. In Japanese, *Ki-bei* means "returning to America." It was the name given to those who were born in the United States but largely educated in Japan. Many Issei wanted to pass on to their children a love for the ancestral homeland. So in some families, children were sent back to Japan where they usually lived with relatives and went to local schools.

In that, the Japanese were not much different from other immigrant groups retaining strong ties to their native land. But Japan in the 1930s had a rigid educational system that taught militaristic values and extreme nationalism.

So the Kibei were often blamed for the disturbances that periodically rocked the camps. Since some Kibei were actively pro-Japan and had been thoroughly indoctrinated by their education, all Kibei were branded as disloyal. Before the outbreak of the war, federal authorities viewed them as a potentially dangerous group. After removal to the camps, the Kibei continued to be suspected as subversives. They were doubly victimized—first by forced evacuation and internment, and then by unfairly being suspected of disloyalty within the camps.

But trouble within the camps was not due to the Kibei. Racist oppression needs no additional motives for revolt.

Minor frictions, disputes with camp authorities, and flare-ups of violence plagued officials. Sometimes the problems were so serious that troops had to be called in to keep order. Confrontations ranged from simple misunderstandings and aggressive behavior of guards to near riots. Sometimes incidents ended in tragedy, as trigger-happy guards shot people who ventured out beyond camp boundaries or otherwise broke rules.

At Topaz, for example, an elderly Issei was shot and killed by a guard. He had approached the camp's outer fence in broad daylight, breaking a rule forbidding aliens to come within a mile of the camp's boundaries. The rule itself was stupid. And all evacuees were fearful that they too might someday be gunned down for some similar harmless offense.

Serious outbreaks were a constant threat. The first took place at the Santa Anita Assembly Center in August 1942. The camp police, made up of evacuees, were making a routine search for forbidden materials. Crowds gathered, angered by the seizure of such essentials as hot plates for cooking, and the carting away of phonograph records and other personal possessions. Police and suspected informers were harassed. The 2,000 protesters were finally dispersed by 200 military policemen.

The Poston camp came closest to open revolt in November 1942, after two suspected informers had been beaten. Camp officials arrested two Kibei and placed them in the camp jail. When evacuee delegations pleaded for the release of the two men—who claimed their innocence—they were told the matter was in the hands of the FBI. Crowds gathered. Issei leaders demanded the men be freed. The community council resigned. Workers went on strike, and the police station was picketed. The demonstrators, mostly Issei, carried banners that resembled the flag of Japan. They threatened violence against *inu* (literally "dogs"), the slang term for informers and for those who worked closely with camp officials).

The protest ended peacefully when Issei leaders realized things were beginning to get out of hand. They set up an emergency council that worked out a compromise. It was agreed that the man charged with assault (the other had been released) would be tried by an evacuee jury. Also, steps would be taken to improve camp conditions and to provide a greater evacuee role in the administration of the camp.

That same month the Heart Mountain, Wyoming, camp was beset with strikes. There was growing friction between evacuee workers hired at low wages and Caucasian staff getting high wages. The strike was broken by shipping the ringleaders to a special detention camp in Arizona. But the next month, 32 evacuees were arrested for breaking security. Their crime? Sledding on a hill outside the camp. Who were they? Children, the oldest of whom was eleven years old. The children's arrest inflamed the residents, who vigorously protested the army's stupidity.

At Manzanar, however, a serious riot erupted in December. It started with the beating of a prominent JACL leader. Several persons were arrested. The beating brought the strong resentment many people felt against the JACL into the open. Its policy of cooperating with the government led many people to view its officials as traitors.

Again, there were mass demonstrations, strikes and protests. Again, militant Issei led the struggle. But at Manzanar there was less of a spirit of compromise on both sides. A secret organization, the Blood Brothers, spearheaded the drive against the JACL and the camp officials. An unruly crowd gathered outside the camp offices while some people rushed off to the camp hospital, intending to attack the victim of the beating again. Hospital authorities hid him, but the mob terrorized hospital staff and patients.

Meanwhile, military policemen on the scene panicked and fired into the crowd. Two people were killed and eight others were wounded. Armed soldiers patrolled the camp and prevented further demonstrations. Then it was learned that extremists had drawn up "death lists," marking several JACL leaders and others friendly to camp authorities for murder.

A sort of peace finally came to the camp when the authorities relocated the people on the death lists. Ringleaders of the protest were arrested and sent to special camps elsewhere. Among these was Joe Kurihara, a Hawaiian Nisei whose leadership of camp militants reflected his bitterness against the nation that had imprisoned him without cause.

Kurihara was a wounded World War I veteran and an active patriot. After Pearl Harbor he tried to volunteer for the armed forces. But he was rejected because of his Japanese ancestry. After internment, he rejected America. "I was wounded fighting for the United States," he said. "These are the scars I have, keepsakes of my army service for this country. It is no longer my country. I am now a hundred percent Japanese. I spit on these scars of the United States."

Because of his outspoken stand, he was the most prominent of the camp dissidents. But many WRA officials understood his fury. One pointed out that Kurihara "is bitter and sore in quite an American way." Another agreed that "if I were Joe Kurihara, I'd be mad too." One of the tragedies of the internment was the waste of the talents of people like Joe Kurihara who could have made a contribution to the nation's war effort and who wanted to be accepted as the loyal Americans they were.

Violence, demonstrations, and tensions were all the inevitable results of unjustly imprisoning masses of people on racial grounds. The upheaval in their lives forced many, like Joe Kurihara, to reject America. It placed some in doubt about their continued faith in this nation. It made others fearful of their future in a hostile country. Added to the natural anger of a pent-up people were the many petty disputes common to camp life and to group living.

So the real question is not why places like Manzanar were hit by riots, but why there were not more such outbreaks. The war, the open hostility of their white neighbors, the loss of their homes and property, the removal to assembly centers, exile to isolated concentration camps, and the hardships of camp life—all placed enormous pressures on the Japanese Americans. That they survived at all is a tribute to their strength and perseverance. That they occasionally gave way to anger and frustration is an acknowledgement of their humanity.

7 Yes-Yes, No-No

From the beginning, the leaders of the War Relocation Authority sought to return the Japanese to normal civilian life. As mentioned earlier, these plans had to be abandoned because of the public's anti-Japanese hysteria.

But the WRA decided to make fresh efforts. It knew that camp life would encourage dependence and that segregation was unhealthy for the Japanese and for the country. Its director, Dillon Myer, had a deeper fear. "We did not want to be responsible," he wrote, "for fostering a new set of reservations in the United States akin to the Indian reservations."

In October 1942, the agency started to encourage evacuees to leave the camps for outside employment. After meeting certain requirements, including a loyalty check,

Dillon Myer, director of the WRA, was anxious to return the evacuees to civilian life and close the camps. He is shown here on a visit to Heart Mountain.

any evacuee could leave the camps. California was still closed, as were some other western states, but the rest of the country was open to them. In fact, the WRA hoped to disperse the Japanese population across the nation.

By the end of 1942, over 800 people had taken advantage of the program. At first, many went to Denver or to Salt Lake City. But local prejudice led the WRA to encourage the evacuees to move further east. The wartime labor shortage helped many towns overcome their hostility to the Japanese, since workers were needed. Chicago alone asked the WRA to help fill 10,000 job openings in mid-1943.

Most of those who left the camps were Nisei, anxious to return to the freedom they had known. The older Issei were more fearful of the outside world. They were less confident of their ability to manage in strange cities far from their former homes.

Even for the more adventurous Nisei, the first taste of freedom was strange. "I was very self-conscious about myself and this feeling didn't disappear for several months," wrote one. "I felt like I was coming out of jail and I thought people stared at me all the time."

Some met with prejudice. There were occasional incidents of assault. Some employers tried to cheat them by paying low wages, thinking that people from the camps wouldn't expect decent treatment. Housing discrimination was also fairly common.

But most people were helpful or indifferent. Quaker and church groups helped organize job and housing opportunities. The WRA established offices in forty-two cities to help convince people to accept the Japanese and to find suitable jobs for them. When the army tried to prevent the Japanese from settling on the East Coast, the WRA got the secretary of war to overrule the military commanders. The WRA also paid the travel fare from the camp to wherever the settler wanted to go. It added some money for living expenses for two weeks.

The WRA felt that the return of the evacuees to civilian life could be speeded up if the army and FBI would take less time with their security clearances. At the same time, the army was going ahead with plans to organize an all-Nisei combat unit. Such a unit was welcomed by many who felt that the citizen Nisei should have the right to fight for their country.

Both of these efforts were aimed at freeing the Japanese

GRETCHEN VAN TASSEL/NATIONAL ARCHIVES
Efforts were made to resettle camp inmates in other parts of the country. Here, WRA officials explain the new policy to an evacuee at the Rohwer camp.

from the camps. But one aspect of each led to tragic results.

It was decided to make all the camp inmates fill out a questionnaire which included a loyalty oath. Some people think that truly disloyal persons will not pledge an oath of loyalty. But that is illogical—such people are the very ones who will be the first to pledge their loyalty. Likewise, it

86

is false to assume that loyal persons will not mind pledging such an oath, since many people of proven loyalty resent being *forced* to take an oath.

Even in the best of times, loyalty oaths are meaningless. But early 1943 was not the best of times. And when people are already under suspicion and being held against their will, forcing them to affirm loyalty can only anger them.

The WRA included loyalty oaths given to Nisei volunteers for the army in a questionnaire which all camp inmates were *required* to fill out in February 1943. The WRA thought that if the evacuees filled out the questionnaire, then the long investigations required for leave clearance could be done away with. Thus, more evacuees could be relocated outside the camps.

But it didn't work that way.

The questionnaire was headed Application for Leave Clearance. Many Issei who did not wish to leave the camps for the unknown wanted nothing to do with it. When camp administrators said everyone had to fill it out, the Issei became confused and resentful.

The heart of the questionnaire lay in questions number 27 and 28. They required simple yes or no answers. Question 27 read: "Are you willing to serve in the armed forces of the United States, in combat duty, wherever ordered?" Question 28 read: "Will you swear unqualified allegiance to the United States of America and faithfully defend the United States from any and all attack by foreign or domestic forces, and forswear any form of allegiance or obedience to the Japanese emperor, or any other foreign government, power, or organization?"

A yes answer to both questions was essential for army recruitment and for leave clearance. A no answer to either one branded a person disloyal and ineligible to leave the camps.

People divided into yes-yes and no-no groups, depending on how they planned to answer the two key questions. All of the pent-up reactions to insults and injustices of the previous months now were focused on the loyalty questions. The bitterness that had been contained now burst forth.

Many Nisei reacted to the questionnaire with fury. One young man who answered yes to both questions was assured by a supervising officer that he was a citizen. Then the young man asked: "May I go to Phoenix?" The officer said no, Phoenix was a banned area. The young man then tore up the questionnaire. "That's the way I feel about your attitude toward our citizenship," he said.

Some Nisei answered no because they feared they'd be forced into the army, perhaps to fight relatives in Japan's army. Others were ordered by their parents to answer no. The no of many others was a protest against the denial of their rights. It was a way of "voting" against the camp officials who forced them to fill out the forms. Togo Tanaka refused to renounce allegiance to the emperor of Japan. Why? Because, he insisted, "we never owed him allegiance. So how could we renounce it? So we refused to sign the stupid questionnaires and we were refused clearance to leave."

The questions were especially unfair to the Issei. Remember that American citizenship was specifically denied by law to people of Japanese birth. Thus the Issei were still citizens of Japan, and it was legally impossible for them to become American citizens. So a yes answer to question 28, which demanded renunciation of Japanese citizenship, would force them to become people without a country. Many Issei feared that if they answered yes, a victorious Japan would punish them. And even if Japan lost the war, it might not allow them to return to retire or to visit.

Later, most camps changed question 28 for the Issei. It now read: "Will you swear to abide by the laws of the United States and to take no action which would in any way interfere with the war effort of the United States?" That made it possible for some to sign. But by the time the question was changed, it was too late to quell the deep anger it had created.

Families were torn by the questions. If Issei answered no-no and their children answered yes-yes, then families might be separated. Many Nisei were thus cruelly asked to choose between their country and their parents.

Results varied from camp to camp. At Minidoka, where special efforts were made to explain the questionnaire and to answer inmates' fears, there were fewer no-no's than at camps like Topaz. There a third of all men answered no-no. And at Manzanar, there was a majority of no-no's.

At Manzanar, questionnaires came on the heels of the December riot and only served to revive the conflicts. Many Issei insisted on being sent back to Japan and pressured their children to answer no-no. At Gila and at Topaz, Nisei and Kibei protesters against the questionnaire were jailed. Some camp administrators told evacuees that they'd be jailed and fined if they refused to answer the questions— an outright lie.

In the end, the answers to the questionnaire proved meaningless. People answered yes or no depending on what they thought the results would mean for them. Some loyal citizens refused to answer yes out of anger or family considerations. Others who might have honestly answered no gave the yes answers the officials wanted. That way they could keep out of trouble or leave the hated camp.

The confusion caused by the questionnaire was evident at the Heart Mountain camp. Prior to February 1943, only 42 persons there had asked to be sent to Japan. In February, when the questionnaires were distributed, 50 more asked to be sent to Japan. In March, 314 made the request. By August, 800 Heart Mountain people wanted to leave for Japan. And a majority of them had answered yes-yes to the loyalty questions!

Every camp was torn by dissension. Fights broke out. Rumors festered. Petitions circulated. Everyone felt that the questionnaires were another move by the government to make their lives unbearable.

One woman wrote, "Bewilderment and confusion was at its height. People walked the roads, tears streaming down their troubled faces, silent and suffering. There were young people stunned and dazed. The little apartments were not big enough for the tremendous battle that raged in practically every room: between parents and children, between America and Japan, between those that were hurt and frustrated, but desperately trying to keep faith in America, and those who were tired and old and disillusioned."

In the end, most people answered yes-yes. Out of 75,000 adults who finally filled out the questionnaire, only about 8,500 answered no-no. Government officials were surprised that more Nisei than Issei were no-no's. But it should not surprise us. The Nisei had learned American principles of citizenship rights and protest. The Issei were more likely to bend to the will of authority. In refusing to answer insulting loyalty oaths, people were actually affirming their American principles. They were expressing their feelings about what had been done to them in the only way open to them.

While the camps were torn over the questionnaire, public opinion was still strongly against the evacuees. Politicians, the press and civic groups kept up a steady drumfire of warnings against letting the Japanese go back to the West Coast.

Kentucky Senator Albert B. Chandler, heading a subcommittee investigating the camps, made highly publicized visits to some of them in March 1943. He helped stir up further anti-Japanese sentiment by claiming that most of the evacuees were disloyal. But his committee's report finally supported the WRA's leave policies.

The House Committee on Un-American Activities also chased after headlines by investigating the evacuation program. Its California hearings in the spring of 1943 brought forth plenty of wild charges against the Japanese. Most fair-minded people agreed with the dissenting report of a committee member who charged that "the report of the majority is prejudiced . . . most of its statements are not proven."

But many people did not need proof. The war against Japan was presented to the public as a racial struggle against "yellow people." California's politicians fed this popular mistrust. Earl Warren, now the state's governor, told a meeting of the National Conference of Governors in June that the Japanese Americans should not be released from the camps. His reason: "No one will be able to tell a saboteur from any other Jap."

Newspaper stories and editorials fostered the belief that the evacuees were living better than most Americans and were surely well off compared to the soldiers at the front. Movies portrayed Nisei spy rings. In *Across the Pacific,* a movie often shown on television today as a Humphrey Bogart classic, a Nisei all-American type turns out to be a treacherous spy plotting to bomb the Panama Canal.

The war was dragging on and people still could not separate the external enemy—Japan—from the Japanese

Americans in the WRA camps. Despite this, the WRA tried to help move the Japanese back into the mainstream of American life. Resettlement efforts continued, even expanded with the final sorting out of the evacuees through the answers to the questionnaires.

But those ineligible to leave the camps on work release—the no-no's—posed a problem. Politicians, the press, and the public branded them disloyal. A Senate resolution demanded they be removed from the camps, where they might "infect" the others, and placed in a segregation center. Even the JACL, spokesmen for the Nisei, favored such a move.

The WRA agreed. Camp officials wanted to get rid of the most embittered inmates. They wanted potential troublemakers sent elsewhere. It was decided that all evacuees who wanted to go to Japan and who had answered no-no, and the family members who chose to stay with them, would be sent to the Tule Lake camp. It was now called the Tule Lake Segregation Center.

Tule Lake was chosen because it was large enough to accommodate the so-called disloyals. It also had large numbers of people who qualified for segregation. During the summer of 1943, the camp was converted into a maximum security facility. An eight-foot barbed wire fence was constructed. New barracks were built to house a guard detachment of 1,000 soldiers. Six tanks were ranged along the military area to warn evacuees of the government's power.

In September, trains began the month-long shuttle to and from Tule Lake. They transported 6,000 "loyal" Tuleans to other camps and brought 9,000 "disloyals" to replace them at the center. For these people, it was the third uprooting in a little over a year. First they were forced into

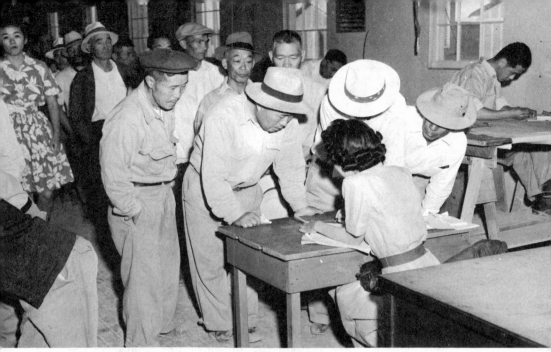

FRANCIS STEWART/NATIONAL ARCHIVES
Evacuees in some of the camps requested repatriation to Japan.

About 9,000 people were labeled "disloyal" and moved to the Tule Lake center from other camps. Signs were posted to welcome the weary new arrivals.

CHARLES E. MACE/NATIONAL ARCHIVES

assembly centers, then to the camps, and now to or away from Tule Lake. Many "loyal" Tuleans refused to move again and insisted on staying in the center. By the spring of 1944, 18,000 people lived there, including many who were not "disloyal" by WRA standards.

Segregating the "disloyals" removed militants from the other camps. But it also concentrated large numbers of angry people in one camp. This was bound to lead to trouble, and it did.

Some of the new arrivals at Tule Lake were so embittered by the treatment they had received that they became militant Japanese nationalists. They openly backed Japan and tried to make Japanese language and customs dominant at Tule Lake. Japanese-language schools were set up, and people were pressured into attending classes. The schools taught political propaganda. Gangs of rough youths threatened those who resisted going to the schools or who continued to practice American customs.

One young Kibei complained that "the people who came from the other camps are all rough. They shout loudly, 'Banzai to the emperor!' and even the police, it seems, are afraid to cross them. If you are caught at anything like [American] dancing, you are likely to be practically killed."

Even before the reshuffling of evacuees to and from Tule Lake had been completed, the camp was troubled. On October 15, a truck carrying workers to the camp farm overturned, injuring twenty-nine people, one of whom later died.

That led to a protest strike by Tule Lake's farm workers. The WRA brought in over 200 "loyal" workers from other camps to harvest the vegetable crop. But that only made the situation more tense. Extremists led the strikers' negotiating committee. Some of them wanted Tule Lake turned into a camp for those who wanted to be sent to Japan. Other issues had more meaning for the majority of the evacuees—bad food, proportionately more food rations for the WRA's Caucasian staff, bad health care, and resentment against official actions. Behind these complaints lurked the smoldering anger of a people unjustly torn from their civilian lives and forced into the camps.

WRA chief Dillon Myer went to Tule Lake at the beginning of November. He found himself at the center of a mass demonstration of over 5,000 evacuees who surrounded the camp's offices. There was violence too—the head doctor of the hospital was beaten. He had tried to prevent agitators from getting hospital employees to walk off their jobs to attend the demonstration.

Myer refused to give in to the negotiating committee. He questioned whether their demands reflected the true wishes of the 15,000 people then at Tule Lake. The following days were dangerous ones. Some WRA employees quit in fear of, as one said, "a knife against my throat." Others demanded the camp's administrators get tough with the evacuees. A fence was begun to separate the employees' houses and offices from the camp's main area. Army patrols were increased, too.

On November 4 the situation got out of hand. A gang of over 200 toughs armed with bats and clubs fought with WRA employees at the central garage. Another group marched on the camp director's house. The army was called in, and tanks and soldiers entered the camp. Machine guns were set up and the riots swiftly put down.

Once in, the army stayed. Martial law was declared on November 13. That meant the camp was under army control. Normal activities were not permitted, and a strict curfew was enforced. The stockade filled up with new prisoners as the army arrested anyone who challenged its authority. Tule Lake was transformed into an armed fortress.

Then the evacuees called a general strike. They refused to cooperate with military authorities. They asked the Spanish consul, who represented Japan's diplomatic interests, to protest their treatment. Petitions pledging support for the negotiating committee were circulated. The prisoners in the stockade went on a hunger strike.

The combination of tight army control and the paralyzing effects of the general strike plunged the camp into gloom. A Nisei girl said of those days: "After the army came in, I really felt like a prisoner. . . . There were no activities. Everything stopped. We had a curfew. Oh, it was a miserable life. . . . we got baloney for Thanksgiving."

Many evacuees were finally ready to reject the extremists who had led them. An advisory council was formed, and it organized a camp-wide vote on ending the strike and restoring normalcy to Tule Lake. They pledged jobs for all who wanted work and promised to get the prisoners held in the stockade released.

In a secret ballot on January 11, the evacuees voted to end the strike by the narrow margin of 4,593 to 4,120. The extremists, calling themselves the Nippon Patriotic Society, challenged the outcome. They claimed that force was used and the results rigged by the army. But the vote accomplished its objective: Martial law was ended. The army withdrew to its base just outside the camp's fence, and the WRA again took control of Tule Lake.

That wasn't the end of troubles at the camp, however. The advisory committee could not deliver on its promises of jobs. Some 350 prisoners were still kept in the stockade under army control. The committee had to disband.

Violent incidents continued. Gangs of extremists beat

up suspected informers. On May 24, 1944, an army sentry provoked an argument with a Nisei truck driver and shot him dead. Eyewitnesses testified that the sentry murdered the man in cold blood, but the sentry was acquitted. In July, a prominent leader of the moderates was murdered. Camp extremists hailed the murder of the man they called Number One Public *Inu,* or informer. Threats of further killings made other moderates afraid to cooperate with the WRA.

Extremist groups, underground until the summer of 1944, now came into the open. They drilled in military formations, shouted pro-Japan slogans, and intensified language training and adoption of Japanese customs. By the fall of 1944, they controlled camp life.

Under the WRA's nose, Tule Lake had entered a reign of terror. Evacuees were not protected by the camp's administrators. They were bitter, left to the rule of a militant, hysterical faction. As we shall see, this led to injustices continuing long after the war had ended.

The turmoil that rocked Tule Lake was felt beyond the camp's fence. The November strike made news all over the country. There were headlines like the Los Angeles *Examiner*'s "14,000 Japs on Strike in State! Army Guarding Fenced-in Nips at Tule Lake." Politicians made headlines with well-publicized charges that the WRA was "too soft." The Japanese government announced it would reconsider its treatment of its American prisoners because of the way the Japanese Americans were being mistreated. After the war, an American prisoner in the Philippines testified that conditions became worse at that time.

But as public attention was concentrated on a relatively small number of justifiably bitter and angry people at Tule Lake, other Japanese Americans were spilling their blood in America's defense on the battlefields of Europe and Asia.

8 "Go For Broke!"

After the attack on Pearl Harbor, Nisei who attempted to enlist in the armed forces were turned away from recruiting stations. Those already in the service were shifted to noncombat posts. One Nisei soldier recalled that "they took the gun away from most of us and replaced it with a broom or a mop, a pencil or a typewriter." Nisei stationed on the West Coast were transferred to other parts of the country, and many were simply discharged. In June 1942, Nisei were not accepted for the draft.

One section of the armed forces, however, wanted Japanese American recruits. The Army Intelligence Service needed men who could speak Japanese to serve as scouts and as interpreters in the Pacific War. Ironically, the Nisei were so thoroughly Americanized that only a tenth of the first 3,700 interviewed knew enough Japanese to be accepted into the service.

A language school was set up in Minnesota, and Nisei were recruited for an intensive study program. It covered the customs, language, and military procedures of Japan. The program was a rugged course of study, and many dropped out. But the school's graduates served with distinction to the end of the war, questioning prisoners and translating captured documents and battle plans. About 3,700 Nisei served in Pacific combat areas, while another 2,300 worked with home-front intelligence units and government information services.

Their efforts helped save countless lives. The Japanese military were so confident that Americans couldn't understand their language that security was loose. Thus, the Nisei became America's "secret weapon." One major coup was the translation of captured documents revealing Japan's plans for the naval battle of the Philippines. When American troops invaded those islands, they knew the complete defense plans of the Japanese Army, thanks to Nisei language and intelligence specialists. The Nisei took part in every landing in the long, grueling American battles along the chain of Pacific islands. After the war ended, they served with the Occupation forces in Japan.

In mid-1942, some government officials urged that the Nisei be allowed to serve in combat forces. The WRA, a prime supporter of such a step, found allies in the government's war propaganda branch, the Office of War Information. The OWI pointed out that Nisei soldiers would help deflate Japan's claims that America was waging a racial war. Assistant Secretary of War John McCloy, one of the major figures behind the evacuation of the Japanese, backed the idea. He said: "It might be well to use our American citizen Japanese . . . where they could be employed against the Germans. I believe we could count on these soldiers to give a good account of themselves."

The JACL wanted the Nisei to be allowed to prove their loyalty by fighting for their country. Its leaders believed that Americans would continue to be suspicious of the Nisei's loyalty unless they proved themselves in combat. While they rejected segregation, they did agree with the army's plans for an all-Nisei outfit. One JACL leader, Mike Masaoka, justified this by saying: "Our thinking was that we were inconspicuous scattered throughout the army. Individual records wouldn't prove much. The army had said Nisei protestations of loyalty were so much hogwash. We had to have a demonstration in blood."

On February 1, 1943, President Roosevelt approved the plan to organize an all-Japanese combat unit. He declared, "No loyal citizen of the United States should be denied the democratic right to exercise the responsibilities of his citizenship, regardless of his ancestry.

"The principle on which this country was founded and by which it has always been governed is that Americanism is a matter of the mind and heart.

"Americanism is not, and never was, a matter of race or ancestry."

While those words helped get the all-Nisei combat unit off the ground, there was a hollow ring to them. Over 100,000 people of Japanese ancestry, including the young men who were expected to fight, were at that very moment under armed guard in the WRA camps.

Once the president gave the army the green light, recruiting teams were sent to the camps to sign up Nisei

100

"No loyal citizen of the United States should be denied the democratic right to exercise the responsibilities of his citizenship, regardless of his ancestry.

"The principle on which this country was founded and by which it has always been governed is that Americanism is a matter of the mind and heart.

"Americanism is not, and never was, a matter of race or ancestry.

"Every loyal American citizen should be given the opportunity to serve this country wherever his skills will make the greatest contribution—whether it be in the ranks of our armed forces, war production, agriculture, government service, or other work essential to the war effort."

THE PRESIDENT OF THE UNITED STATES, FEBRUARY 3, 1943

NATIONAL ARCHIVES
Government antidiscrimination poster, part of a campaign to fight the prejudice encountered by evacuees who had left the camps for other parts of the United States.

volunteers. Members of the teams were thoroughly briefed. They had a prepared speech written in Washington for them. It stressed that millions of Americans disagreed with the forced evacuation. It said that the recruiting effort showed the nation's intention "to go further in restoring to you a normal place in the life of the country." They also prepared for the expected hot questions, but many were unanswerable.

Evacuees wanted to know why Japanese Americans in the armed forces had been dismissed or reduced to performing menial tasks. They asked why the navy refused to accept Nisei. Why would the planned unit be segregated? Why did the recruiting teams include so few Nisei? Why were Nisei in uniform not allowed to return to the West Coast on furlough? Above all, they asked, if army service would prove loyalty, why had the Japanese veterans of the First World War been thrown into the camps?

The recruiters also faced the deep hostility brought about by the loyalty questionnaire. As mentioned in chapter seven, one of the purposes of the questionnaire was to help determine loyalty for leave clearances, including army service.

About a quarter of the Nisei answered the loyalty questions in a way that disqualified them for volunteering for the army. Many of the Issei urged their children not to volunteer. But others, following traditional Japanese concepts of duty and loyalty to the land in which one lived, spoke up strongly in favor of volunteering. One Issei told a meeting at the Minidoka camp:

"Let the Nisei do their duty toward the country in which they were born and to which they have allegiance. . . . The principle involved is that since our children were born here, they belong here. Morally speaking, they do not be-

102

long to us, but to their country. I believe our attitude towards this principle will be extremely important for the future welfare and happiness of our own race in the United States. We should look to our own moral code in this matter.''

But in some camps, hostility was so great that recruits had to be spirited out of camp for their own protection. There were strong pressures on young Nisei to stay on in the camps. The recruiting effort was a flop. The army got only about 1,200 Nisei volunteers from the camps—about a third of the number expected.

The all-Japanese fighting unit, the 442nd Regimental Combat Team, was patched together. It was made up of camp volunteers, Hawaiian Japanese recruits, and Nisei already serving in the army. Another fighting outfit of Japanese Americans, the 100th Infantry Battalion, was an all-Nisei Hawaiian National Guard battalion that was federalized after Pearl Harbor and shipped stateside.

Both units were sent to Camp Shelby, Mississippi, in the spring of 1943, for intensive combat training. From the start, it became obvious that the Nisei would become an elite unit. In mock battle exercises, they consistently wiped out larger opposition forces. The average IQ of the men of the 442nd was higher than that required for admission to officer training programs. Above all, they were men with a mission. They saw their service as the opportunity to win freedom for their families and to wipe the stain of suspicion from the Japanese American community.

Their regimental motto, Go for Broke, reflected this. Originally, it was a phrase used by dice shooters that meant ''to go all out.'' One member of the 442nd, Daniel Inouye, later to become a U.S. senator, said Go for Broke meant: ''to give everything we did, everything we had; to jab every bayonet dummy as though it were a living, breathing Nazi; to scramble over an obstacle course as though our lives depended on it; to march quick-time until we were ready to drop, and then to break into a trot.''

Camp Shelby was near Hattiesburg, Mississippi, and in 1943 that town, like the rest of the South, was rigidly segregated. All public facilities—movies, restaurants, waiting rooms, buses and trains—had separate sections for whites and blacks. For most of the Nisei, it was their first experience with that kind of racial segregation. They were not pleased when their commander announced that ''during your time in this state, you will be treated by its people as white men.'' They were ordered to respect local customs and not break the color line by sitting in the black sections of movie houses and buses.

This was a bitter pill. Victims of racism themselves, the Nisei couldn't stomach their ''honorary white'' status. But they followed orders. Disciplined as the Nisei were, however, soldiers from other units who threw racial slurs at them learned to regret it. When one unit passed through Camp Shelby and called the Nisei ''Japs,'' Inouye reports that unit ''accumulated quite a collection of black eyes and fat lips by the time they shipped out.''

The 100th Infantry Battalion, well advanced in its training, was the first to see action. In September 1943, it landed in North Africa and took part in the bloody fighting in the invasion of Italy. It suffered so many casualties that it had to be reinforced by men from the 442nd. The rest of the 442nd was thrown into action in the Italian campaign in June 1944.

The arrival of Nisei troops proved confusing for other Americans as well as for the enemy. All officers of the Fifth Army in Italy were alerted that the 442nd would be

Volunteers of the all-Nisei infantry battalion, shown here on the way to the Italian front in 1943, won a reputation for bravery.

at the front, that its soldiers were proud of "their American origin." Officers were told to alert their troops "in order that . . . cases of mistaken identity may be avoided."

The enemy, of course, was not alerted, and when the 442nd took its first prisoners, the Germans and Italians were astonished. None of them could figure out what Japanese soldiers were doing in American uniforms, fighting Japan's allies. One German soldier asked his captors if Japan had deserted the Axis cause.

The excellent fighting record compiled by the Nisei led the War Department to make all Nisei subject to the draft, just as other young Americans had been. But even this decision, long sought by the WRA and the JACL, was marred. Prospective inductees were required to fill out a questionnaire different from that given non-Japanese. It asked for detailed information about their background, family, and ties to Japan. It also obliged them to sign a statement forswearing obedience to Japan and pledging loyalty to the United States.

The announcement that the Nisei would be drafted was made in January 1944. It set off another shock wave through some of the camps. Several hundred refused to be inducted into the armed forces, and many were jailed. In one case, a federal judge ruled the government could not draft them from camps in which they were being held against their will. "It is shocking to the conscience," wrote Judge Louis Goodman, "that an American citizen be confined on the ground of disloyalty, and then, while so under duress and restraint, be compelled to serve in the armed forces or be prosecuted for not yielding to such compulsion."

But his was a lone voice. Other courts convicted draft resisters. It wasn't until President Truman granted amnesty for all wartime draft offenses in December 1947 that their full citizenship rights were restored.

By spring 1944, the mood had changed within many of the camps, and there were relatively few instances of draft resistance. Most Nisei willingly answered the call to duty. In contrast to their reactions to the previous year's army recruiting efforts, parents and peers of the Nisei urged them to join the army. In one camp, draftees leaving for the army were given a small cash gift and their neighbors' best wishes in a ceremony led by the elders of the camp.

The draftees were earmarked as replacements to keep the 100th Infantry Battalion and the 442nd Regimental

Combat Team at full strength. And replacements were needed, for those all-Nisei units took a fearful pounding in front-line fighting. Just a few months after landing in Italy, men of the 100th had earned over 1,000 Purple Hearts, the medal given to those wounded in battle. They won 74 decorations for especially heroic deeds. By mid-1944, the 100th became a part of the 442nd, which spearheaded the American drive up the spine of Italy, facing crack German troops.

The Nisei units fought their way from Rome to Florence before they were pulled out of Italy and sent to France. There, in October, the 442nd was thrown into the bitter battle of the Vosges mountains. German troops were engaged in a bitter, last-ditch stand to hold off the Allies. There was heavy fighting in mined, wooded areas blanketed by enemy fire. The Nisei were assigned to relieve the "Lost Battalion," a Texas unit that was trapped behind enemy lines. The Texans had been caught for a week in a pocket circled by German machine gun and mortar fire. The men of the 442nd slogged through rain and muddy ground, fighting all the way and taking heavy losses. Finally, they broke through the German cordon and saved the beleaguered troops.

It was a glorious feat, one of the high points of the war in Western Europe, but it was bought at a high cost. The 442nd suffered a 60 percent casualty rate, losing more than the 300 men who were saved.

After this, the 442nd spent some time in a fairly quiet zone. Then they went back to Italy for the final push that drove the Germans out of that country. The Nisei fighters again did the impossible. This time they wiped out German positions that had beaten off American attacks for five months.

Because it was an elite fighting unit pressed into the heaviest action, and because of its Go for Broke spirit, the 442nd had one of the highest casualty rates in the army. It suffered over 9,000 dead and wounded, more than three times its original strength. Many men were wounded several times and rejoined the unit, to be wounded again.

Although it was a relatively small unit, the 442nd won enough decorations for two divisions. These included 7 Presidential Unit Citations and a Congressional Medal of Honor, 52 Distinguished Service Crosses, and 560 Silver Stars. Its men piled up 18,143 individual decorations! After the war, Texas made all members of the 442nd honorary citizens of the state, in appreciation for the rescue of the Lost Battalion.

Although most Americans were familiar with the Nisei's role in the fighting in Europe, their important service in the Pacific battles was less publicized. In part, that was because they were spread among many units and because most were translators and interpreters. But even in such positions, the Nisei were in the thick of combat, joining infantry patrols and taking part in hand-to-hand fighting. Nisei scouts overheard orders given by Japanese commanders and alerted their units to concentrate their defense on places they knew the Japanese would be attacking. One Nisei, with the famous Merrill's Marauders, earned the nickname Horizontal Hank because of the many times he was pinned down by enemy machine gun fire. One of his comrades wrote home:

"Many of the boys, and myself especially, never knew a Japanese American or what one was like. . . . Now we know and the Marauders want you to know that they are backing the Nisei 100 percent. It makes the boys and myself raging mad to read about movements against the Japanese Americans by the 4-F'ers back home. We would dare them to say things like they have in front of us.''

Kenny Yasui, a Kibei, pretended to be a Japanese colonel and captured sixteen enemy soldiers, ordering them to drop their weapons and march off to commands he remembered from his student days in Tokyo. Ben Kuroki, a Nisei from Nebraska, was an air force gunner on bombers. He flew thirty combat missions—five more than required—before refusing a soft stateside post in order to continue flying, this time in the Pacific. He wound up with fifty-eight combat missions and three coveted decorations. He helped break the prejudice against the Nisei through a well publicized speech in San Francisco. There he spoke of the similarity of the battle against the Axis abroad and intolerance at home. ''We will have lost the war if our military victory is not followed by a better understanding among peoples,'' he said.

Ben was one of four Kuroki brothers serving with the armed forces. The Masaoka family had five sons serving in the same combat unit. And the Nakada family had nine sons on active duty.

Stories of personal valor and of Nisei heroism were spread across the country by War Department press releases. The department, which had stripped Japanese Americans of their rights, was now trying, through publicity, to overcome anti-Japanese prejudice. Columnists and magazines, including some that had called for evacuation, now ran stories about the Purple Heart Battalion and praised the Nisei's fighting spirit. To such voices were added those of soldiers writing their hometown papers to counter anti-Japanese American letters or editorials.

The government may have been hypocritical in cranking out press releases about the superb job the Nisei were doing while keeping their families behind barbed wire. But it was clear that the gamble many Nisei soldiers made did pay off. They thought that by distinguishing themselves in combat they would be better able to win acceptance.

And that is what happened. The answer to those who charged Japanese Americans with disloyalty was given on the battlefields by the bloody sacrifices of the Nisei. As Mike Masaoka said after the war: "We were probably the only group of American soldiers in World War II who got what we fought for."

At the war's end, tributes flowed in to the returning veterans. President Truman personally awarded the 442nd their seventh Presidential Unit Citation after a parade through the capitol. He told them: "You fought not only the enemy, but you fought prejudice and you have won."

But that fight was far from over. Ernest Uno returned from his years of combat to find his mother still in a camp. Their meeting, in the visitor's cottage, had to be in the presence of an armed guard.

In 1947, Dan Inouye, who had bicycled to the field hospital to help out when Pearl Harbor was bombed, was a U.S. Army captain. After two years in a hospital recovering from his wounds, he was ready to go home to Hawaii. First, he decided to get a haircut. In his autobiography, *Journey to Washington,* he tells what happened:

" 'Are you Chinese?' the man said to me.

"I looked past him at the three empty chairs, the other two barbers watching us closely. 'I'm an American,' I said.

" 'Are you Chinese?'

" 'I think what you want to know is where my father was born. My father was born in Japan. I'm an American.' Deep in my gut I knew what was coming.

The fighting exploits of the Nisei soldiers helped overcome the racial prejudice that put Japanese Americans into the camps. Here, the 442nd Regiment returns home after the war.

" 'Don't give me that American stuff,' he said swiftly. 'You're a Jap and we don't cut Jap hair.'

"I wanted to hit him. I could see myself—it was as though I were standing in front of a mirror. There I stood, in full uniform, the new captain's bars bright on my shoulders, four rows of ribbons on my chest, the combat infantry badge, the distinguished unit citations—and a hook where my hand was supposed to be. And he didn't cut Jap hair. To think that I had gone through a war to save his skin—and he didn't cut Jap hair.

"I said, 'I'm sorry for you and the likes of you.' And I went back to my ship."

9 The Courts

While the men of the 442nd were spilling their blood on the hills of Italy and in the forests of France, lawyers were arguing the rights of Japanese Americans in the courts.

The young Nisei in uniforms were fighting to gain acceptance from other Americans. The lawyers were battling to win freedom for the inmates of the camps. They challenged the constitutionality of the government's exclusion of the Japanese from the West Coast, their removal to guarded camps, and the denial of their rights.

The Constitution reserves great powers for the federal government in time of war. There was no question in anyone's mind that the government had the legal power to draft people into the armed forces or to otherwise limit some freedoms.

CHARLES E. MACE/NATIONAL ARCHIVES
Persons of Japanese ancestry—but not aliens from other countries—were held in relocation centers. This sign was posted on the Tule Lake boundary.

But there was doubt about its right to force people from their homes and to keep them in camps. The lawyers working for the Japanese Americans asked the courts to rule that the government had overstepped its powers and had violated the Constitution.

One issue they raised was the discriminatory character of the evacuation orders. Only the Japanese Americans were evacuated and held against their will. Others, even aliens from countries with whom we were also at war, Germany and Italy, were not given similar treatment.

114

A second issue was the extent to which the military could control the civilian population. This was something that had come up before in our history, during the Civil War. In 1864 the Union Army arrested a man named Milligan, tried him in a military court, and sentenced him to death. Milligan claimed the military did not have the power to put a civilian on trial and to sentence him. In 1866 the Supreme Court supported his position. It said that although he had been arrested in a war zone, Milligan had the right to a civilian trial, with a judge and jury as the Constitution provides. The military might take some limited steps in a time of emergency. For example, it might detain a citizen for a while. But no crisis could justify suspension of constitutional guarantees for a civilian trial by jury.

The Japanese Americans and their lawyers hoped the courts would uphold the principles laid down in the *Milligan* case. They said the government and the military had no legal power to discriminate against the Japanese and to keep them in the camps. We may be at war with Japan, they argued, but, as the *Milligan* case established, the Constitution still protects citizens.

Their point dealt with the Nisei and the Kibei who, as American citizens, had rights the government could not infringe. The Issei were in a different legal situation. No one seriously questioned the right of the government to detain citizens of a nation with whom it was at war.

The evacuation was a blatant violation of constitutional rights. Many government officials and military men were doubtful they had the power to order it. In the early days of the war, the Justice Department was very careful to proceed according to legal limits. Attorney General Biddle finally turned over the "Japanese problem" to the military because he did not have the power to detain persons suspected of disloyalty. Even Provost Marshall General Gullion thought martial law would have to be declared before any evacuation program was begun. General De Witt was worried about court interference with the evacuation.

But it wasn't until 1943 that the first major challenge to the government's actions reached the Supreme Court. This was the case of Gordon Hirabayashi, a Nisei who violated the curfew. He was sentenced to three months imprisonment. He said the conviction should be overturned because the curfew was an act of racial discrimination and a violation of his civil rights. On June 21, 1943, a unanimous Supreme Court upheld his conviction.

"We cannot close our eyes to the fact," the Court said, "that in time of war, residents having ethnic affiliations with an invading enemy may be a greater source of danger than those of a different ancestry."

It was a curious decision. Some members of the Court noted for their devotion to civil liberties voted to uphold Hirabayashi's conviction. And they based that judgment on clearly unconstitutional racial grounds.

In a concurring opinion, Justice William O. Douglas stated: "I think it is important to emphasize that we are dealing here with a problem of loyalty, not assimilation. Loyalty is a matter of mind and of heart, not of race. That indeed is the history of America. Moreover, guilt is personal under our constitutional system."

Then, after writing those exemplary words, he, like the others, voted in favor of a decision that made race the reason for depriving an American of his rights. Why?

The proceedings of the Supreme Court are shrouded in secrecy. After a case is argued in court, the justices meet in private to discuss it. Opinions are written, circulated, and often changed to win the votes of other judges. By tradition, the give and take, the arguing back and forth, are never revealed to the public.

116

But we can get a glimpse of the thinking of the Court through the diaries of Justice Felix Frankfurter, which were published after his death. In an entry dated June 5, 1943, Frankfurter recorded some of the Court's secret conversations about the *Hirabayashi* case.

Frankfurter said that Douglas's concurring opinion was "full of cheap oratory about America winning the war and all that sort of stuff." Justice Hugo Black, a staunch civil libertarian, told his colleagues that "in time of war somebody has to exercise authority and he did not think the courts could review anything the military does." Black continued, admitting that "if he were the commanding general, he would not let the evacuated Japanese come back even if the Court directed that to be done."

Frankfurter reported that he and Justice Owen Roberts tried to get all nine justices to agree on a joint position. He had trouble with Justice Frank Murphy, "who still has worries about drawing the line on the score of what he calls 'ancestry.' " Justice Black suggested that because of discrimination against the Japanese, they might be tempted to be disloyal if allowed to return to the West Coast. That justified the military orders against them, Black said. "Even if that is true," he went on, "I do not think it should be said because I am against saying anything that may give the propagandists of our enemies a lift."

Thus the Frankfurter diaries give us a shocking picture of a Supreme Court openly backing discriminatory and dictatorial steps. The justices were swept by the same passions as lesser citizens. They were slavish in upholding the military's abuse of power. By abdicating their responsibility to defend the Constitution, the Supreme Court became just another cog in the war machine.

Observers of the Court felt that as the war news got better, the Court's decisions would improve. The *Hirabay-*

ashi decision came at a time when no Allied soldiers had yet arrived in continental Western Europe. And American troops were still bogged down in a brutal campaign in the South Pacific.

In 1944, the situation changed drastically. American soldiers liberated France and were headed for the German heartlands. In the Pacific, the Japanese suffered heavy air and naval losses and were clearly doomed to defeat. It was in that more favorable atmosphere that the *Korematsu* and *Endo* cases, challenging the continued internment of Japanese Americans, came to the Supreme Court.

Fred Korematsu was a Nisei whose plans to marry a Caucasian girl were threatened by the evacuation order. He changed his name, altered his features through plastic surgery, and went into hiding to avoid being sent to a camp. The FBI arrested him for remaining in a prohibited zone. He asked that the Court overturn his conviction on the grounds that the evacuation orders were unconstitutional.

The American Civil Liberties Union said the issue in the case was "whether or not a citizen of the United States may, because he is of Japanese ancestry, be confined in barbed-wire stockades euphemistically termed assembly centers or relocation centers—actually concentration camps."

The *Hirabayashi* case concerned the government's right to enforce a curfew for specific groups of people. The *Korematsu* case now questioned the government's right to order the evacuation of a specific group. Do the military and the government have the right to evacuate people on the grounds of ancestry? Sadly, on December 18, 1944, the Supreme Court answered yes.

The majority of the Court decided that when orders were implemented in 1942, there was "the gravest imminent danger to the public safety." It had accepted the military's view of the situation, a view not borne out by facts. But that brought the Court face to face with the long-standing legal principle applied to *Milligan*—that the government's war powers do not suspend basic constitutional rights.

The Court swept that consideration aside. Justice Black's opinion for the majority declared:

"In the light of the principles we announced in the *Hirabayashi* case, we are unable to conclude that it was beyond the war power of Congress and the Executive to exclude those of Japanese ancestry from the West Coast area at the time they did."

The judges even pretended that racial discrimination was not a factor in the exclusion. Justice Douglas actually stated in his concurring opinion that "Korematsu was not excluded from the Military Area because of hostility to him or his race." Douglas was offended by terming the relocation camps "concentration camps," and he said, "we are dealing specifically with nothing but an exclusion order."

Some members of the Court could no longer swallow such mockery of basic constitutional principles. The Court split, 6–3. Justices Murphy, Jackson and Roberts said the exclusion orders were unconstitutional.

Justice Roberts wrote that "it is a case of convicting a citizen as punishment for not submitting to imprisonment in a concentration camp, based on his ancestry, and solely on his ancestry, without evidence or inquiry concerning his loyalty and good disposition towards the United States. . . . I need hardly labor the conclusion that constitutional rights have been violated."

Another dissenter, Justice Murphy, condemned "this racial restriction which is one of the most sweeping and complete deprivations of constitutional rights in the history of this nation in the absence of martial law.'' He called the decision a "legalization of racism.''

Despite the eloquence of the dissenters, the Court ruled that the government had the power to exclude the Japanese from the West Coast. But having done so, did it have the power to keep them in the camps? That was the crucial issue in the third and last of the cases before the Court, that of Mitsuye Endo. It was decided on the same day as the *Korematsu* case: December 18, 1944.

Mitsuye Endo was a twenty-two-year-old stenographer for the state of California when, in 1942, she was evacuated to Tule Lake. Her lawyers did not challenge the government's right to exclude her from the West Coast. But they denied its right to keep loyal citizens in the camps.

Government lawyers were quite certain the Supreme Court would rule that Endo's rights were violated by continued detention. They urged the WRA to release her, even though she refused to apply for leave clearance. WRA director Dillon Myer refused. He wanted Endo to win the case, ''in order that we might abolish any further need for leave regulations for anyone like Miss Endo who was free to relocate.''

This time, the Court could not justify detention of a loyal citizen. All nine justices voted that Miss Endo had to be freed. But the Court's majority still firmly refused to face the real issues.

Justice Douglas wrote that although ''Mitsuye Endo should be given her liberty . . . we do not come to the underlying constitutional issues which have been argued.'' Instead of ruling that the government's detention orders were unconstitutional, Douglas found only that the WRA ''has no authority to subject citizens who are concededly loyal to its leave procedure.''

120

The fault, the Court was saying, was not with a racially based exclusion and detention system, but with the WRA's leave regulations.

Justices Murphy and Roberts joined the majority in deciding Miss Endo should be released. But they filed opinions that sharply rebuked the other justices. Justice Murphy argued that "detention in relocation centers of persons of Japanese ancestry regardless of loyalty is . . . another example of the unconstitutional resort to racism inherent in the entire evacuation program."

So, while the Court sidestepped the constitutional questions of the government's powers to hold citizens against their will in wartime, it did free Mitsuye Endo. Such decisions do not apply only to individuals. They apply to a whole group of people in similar situations. Thus, when the Court ruled the curfew and evacuation legal, it meant that the government had the right to restrict not only Hirabayashi and Korematsu, but all of the people affected by those orders. Now, in freeing Endo, it also freed all loyal Japanese Americans still in the camps.

The "Japanese cases" constitute one of the Supreme Court's darkest hours. Supposed to be the citizen's main line of defense against abuse of constitutional rights, the Court had turned itself into an arm of the military. It backed suspension of basic civil rights, allowed capricious military judgments to go unchallenged, and upheld racially discriminatory acts. When it finally ordered the release of loyal citizens from the camps, it did so on the narrowest possible grounds. It did not even begin to deal with the core constitutional questions raised by the establishment of concentration camps.

The *Endo* decision, requiring the WRA to release its charges, came as no surprise to government officials. By 1944, officials were trying to decide not *whether* the Japanese should be released from the camps, but how and when.

In May 1944, Chief of Staff General George C. Marshall told the War Department that the military had only one concern about returning the Japanese to the West Coast. If they become targets of violence there, the Japanese government might retaliate against American prisoners of war. Marshall added, "There are, of course, strong political reasons why the Japanese should not be returned to the West Coast before next November."

This was a reference to the coming presidential election. President Roosevelt did not want to take any steps, such as freeing the Japanese, that might lose him votes in the key state of California.

In June, Roosevelt opposed "anything drastic," such as "suddenly ending the orders excluding Japanese Americans from the West Coast." He suggested that the government determine "how many Japanese families would be acceptable to public opinion in definite localities on the West Coast." And he wanted to "extend greatly the distribution of other [Japanese American] families in many parts of the United States." Roosevelt was sure that the rest of the country would accept the dispersed Japanese— "one or two families to each county as a start."

Roosevelt's reelection in November smoothed the way for the release of the Japanese Americans, since there was no longer a fear of antagonizing California's voters. Meanwhile, the *Korematsu* and *Endo* cases were due to be decided. Officials were sure the Court would not allow further detention of the Japanese in the camps. In December, Secretary of War Stimson told Roosevelt that "in view of the fact that military necessity no longer requires the continuation of mass exclusion, it seems unlikely that it can be continued in effect for any considerable period."

One day before the Court delivered its opinion in the *Endo* case, Major General Henry C. Pratt, now chief of the Western Defense Command, announced that loyal Japanese Americans would be allowed to go back to the West Coast. On December 18 came the *Endo* decision that would require the WRA to release the evacuees. The same day, the WRA announced that all of the camps would be closed by the end of 1945.

The long ordeal of America's Japanese was finally about to end.

10 Going Home

By Christmas 1944, 35,000 people had already left the camps—some to join the armed forces, some through WRA leave clearance. Large numbers of the latter group had relocated to other parts of the country. The Jerome camp had closed in mid-1944.

Aside from the no-no group, many of the 85,000 people still in the camps were elderly Issei.

The announcement of the camp closings set off a rush of requests for leave. In December 1944, only 535 people left the camps. In January that figure doubled, and then it doubled again in February. Each month saw more people leaving. By September 1945, 15,000 people a month were moving out of the camps.

124

Newly released evacuees take a final view of Jerome Center from one of its guard towers.

125

The camps were becoming ghost towns, with those left behind generally those most fearful of the outside world. Some of the Issei resisted losing the security the camps provided in what appeared to be a hostile world. But most thought that younger people should leave. One WRA staff member at Poston wrote: "There is a growing feeling in some Issei circles that there's just a little something wrong with a young person who is still in the center."

The WRA emptied the camps as quickly as possible. Camps were shut down steadily throughout 1945 until only Tule Lake remained. It was home to 7,000 people, most of whom were not eligible for leave because they had renounced their citizenship.

Some people refused to go. The government had torn them from their homes and put them in camps. Now, they felt, it intended to turn them loose without adequately providing housing, jobs, and other means of becoming independent.

The WRA could not totally ignore the drumfire of evacuee protests against the sudden closings of the camps. It called an all-center conference at Salt Lake City in February 1945. There, camp delegates tried to get the WRA to provide assistance for people leaving the centers. They drew up a long list of grievances. They pointed out the mental suffering and financial losses inflicted on the evacuees, and their fears of prejudice and violence on returning to their former homes. Many of the elderly Issei depended on their sons for support, and those sons were now away in the armed forces. They asked for federal help to find homes at a time of severe housing shortage. Many of the evacuees who had not sold their farms and homes outright had leased them when they went to the camps, and so they had nothing to return to.

During 1945 the camps emptied and the Japanese Americans returned to their former homes. Before leaving Poston, men and women stand in line for ration books, and a child takes a last look.

But the WRA gave the conferees the cold shoulder. The evacuees would have to relocate on their own, with minimum assistance from the government. Bad as this news was, it was preferable to the rumor-laden confusion that had gripped the camps.

Gloom spread throughout the communities of older people. As one elderly Issei wrote: "We are told and encouraged to relocate again into the world as a stranger in strange communities! We now have lost all security. WRA urges readjustment, relocating outside. Where shall we go? What shall we do at the twilight of the evening of our lives?"

Rumors spread that evacuees returning to California had been beaten or even murdered. The early months of 1945 were a time of carefully testing the situation on the West Coast. The "scouts"—early returnees—wrote back to friends still in the camps that they had not experienced ugly incidents and were reestablishing themselves. Then the rumors slowed to a trickle, and more people returned to the West Coast.

The fear of violence was not irrational. In January alone, there were thirty incidents of terrorism against returning Japanese Americans in California. These ranged from an attempted bombing to rifle shots fired at farmhouses to telephoned death threats. Many returned to their old homes to find their farms neglected and made worthless, personal belongings stored in Buddhist temples had been stolen, stores vandalized.

In Hood River, Oregon, the local American Legion post had removed the names of Nisei servicemen from the town's honor roll. Three hundred Hood River residents signed a petition urging that the Japanese be welcomed back. But five hundred signed a newspaper advertisement telling the Japanese they were not wanted. In Oregon and

FRANCIS STEWART / NATIONAL ARCHIVES

On returning from the camps, many found their farms neglected. Others lost goods stored in Buddhist temples, like the one below in Los Angeles, that had been vandalized.

NATIONAL ARCHIVES

Washington, the big packinghouses refused to buy produce from Japanese farmers until other farmers had sold their crops.

Night riders stalked the farming valleys of California, shooting into houses and orchards of Japanese farmers. Hundreds of such incidents were reported. When the terrorists were caught, they often got off lightly. One man who admitted firing shots into the home of a Japanese American got only a suspended sentence.

Less violent harassment was common. Some evacuees would be met by an old neighbor who advised them not to plan on staying because "people here are planning trouble for you Japanese." Some workers refused to work alongside the returnees. In some cities, Japanese were refused sales tax permits or other documents needed to reopen their businesses.

But there were forces working on behalf of the Japanese, too. One national union suspended its West Coast local for excluding Japanese members. In many communities, citizens' groups were organized to assist the returnees, often helping them find housing and easing their way back to civilian life.

The achievements of the 442nd helped many people to overcome their anti-Japanese American prejudices. A hero of the Pacific War, General Joseph (Vinegar Joe) Stilwell, came to California to award the Distinguished Service Cross to the family of a Nisei who had died in combat. The family had earlier been driven from their home by night-riding terrorists.

Many agreed with General Stilwell when he said: "The Nisei bought an awful big chunk of America with their blood. . . . I say we soldiers ought to form a pickax club to protect Japanese Americans who fought the war with

130

us. Any time we see a barfly commando picking on these kids or discriminating against them, we ought to bang him over the head with a pickax. I'm willing to be a charter member. We cannot allow a single injustice to be done to the Nisei without defeating the purposes for which we fought."

Movie stars and other celebrities spoke up for acceptance of the Japanese Americans. National offices of veterans groups, including the American Legion, paid tribute to the fine record of the Nisei soldiers. Such favorable publicity helped offset the anti-Japanese diatribes of some newspapers and racist organizations.

By mid-1945, the anti-Japanese agitation tapered off. Some of the political figures who had objected to letting the Japanese return now did an about-face. In 1943, Los Angeles' Mayor Fletcher Bowron had said his city did not want the Japanese Americans to return and that they should be deprived of citizenship. Now he held a public ceremony on the steps of the City Hall for the first group of returnees. "We want you and all other citizens of Japanese ancestry who have relocated here to feel secure in your home," he told them.

The year before, Governor Earl Warren warned that there might be anti-Japanese rioting if they were allowed back in the state. Now he publicly urged Californians to comply "loyally, cheerfully and carefully" with the government's decision. State Attorney General Robert W. Kenney was especially forceful in his condemnation of anti-Japanese incidents and helped set a mood of greater racial tolerance.

Another helpful factor was the San Francisco meeting (April 25 to June 26, 1945) of the United Nations Conference, formed to draw up a charter for the world body. Some of the delegates objected to the city as a site for the meeting because of its record of intolerance. That moved some newspapers to publish editorials about the need to get along with each other if we are to be able to get along with other races in the world.

But the deciding factor in winning acceptance for the returning Japanese was probably the fact that the government had ordered their return. People may still have held their prejudices, but they weren't about to defy governmental authority, especially in wartime.

The returning Japanese found much that had changed. Over a million people migrated to California during the war, attracted by jobs in defense industries. Los Angeles' Japanese enclave, Little Tokyo, was now called Bronzeville and largely populated by blacks. Housing was scarce since the war halted construction of new homes. Land prices were so high that returning farmers could not afford to buy or rent land. Many Issei were back to where they had started decades ago as new arrivals in America.

The Japanese tradition of self-help and mutual aid was an asset. Early returnees helped later arrivals, often putting them up in their own homes until they could find housing. The lucky few who could return to farms or businesses hired their fellow evacuees. Those who had a little money, invested in small boardinghouses and hotels. That helped returnees find housing. The energy and hard work of the Japanese soon reestablished them solidly. By 1946, Little Tokyo was once more alive with Japanese shops and restaurants.

Not all of the Japanese returned to the West Coast. Over 30,000 now lived in the East and the Midwest. Fifteen thousand were in Illinois alone, most of them in Chicago. By 1950, less than 6 out of 10 Japanese Americans lived on the West Coast. Before the war, 9 out of 10 lived there. And by 1970, although over 200,000 people of Japanese ancestry lived in California, almost as many—160,000—lived outside the state.

The evacuation and internment broke the pattern of Japanese settlement in America. Hawaii and California remain centers of Japanese American life. But there are now Japanese living in every state of the Union, with thriving communities in most of the country's major cities. This population dispersal has helped ease the group into the mainstream of American life.

While the other centers were being evacuated, Tule Lake was a hotbed of dissent. It was dominated by a radical group which called for "resegregation." They realized—as the officials did not—that many people at Tule Lake remained loyal to America. The resegregationists wanted to be separated from such neighbors. They wanted to renounce their American citizenship and move to Japan after the war.

By the end of 1944, they had terrorized some evacuees into giving up their citizenship. Some agreed to renounce American citizenship because a family member wanted to go back to Japan. Some renounced it because they saw no future for themselves in postwar America. Some gave it up because they feared being beaten if they refused. And many did so simply because they were confused, like the Nisei who later said: "I was so undecided that any little pressure one way or another swayed my decision."

It is an extraordinary situation for citizens of a nation at war to legally give up their citizenship. Most countries do not allow it. But in mid-1944, Congress passed the Denationalization Act. It allowed any person to give up his American citizenship in wartime simply by making a written declaration of renunciation.

The Justice Department thought the law would enable it

to detain disloyal evacuees if the Supreme Court ordered the camps closed. Instead of just a small group of the emperor's loyalists, thousands of Nisei applied for renunciation of their citizenship. Throughout 1944 and 1945, about 5,700 people—most of them evacuees who were in no state of mind to make such an important decision—sent such applications to the attorney general.

The Justice Department sent hearing officers to try to persuade the renunciants to change their minds and keep their American citizenship. While the hearing officers were sometimes successful, they failed to convince those who feared attacks from the pro-Japan terrorists to withdraw their applications.

A reign of terror engulfed Tule Lake. Rumors spread that families would be broken. This frightened Nisei who thought their Issei parents would be shipped back to Japan without them. As one confessed, "I piled lies upon lies at the renunciation hearing. . . . I didn't mean anything I said at the time, but fear and anxiety was too strong." Another Nisei said, "We had no way of moving out or away from terrorism in this fenced-in concentration camp."

So the renunciation hearings were a flop. They took place among the confused remnant that had lost the ability to make sound decisions. A law designed to make it easier to detain a few hundred disloyal persons trapped thousands of confused people in a situation that left them without a country.

The renunciation hearings took place early in 1945. But it wasn't until March that the Justice Department transferred the extremists out of Tule Lake. About a thousand people were sent to smaller camps. That restored some normality to Tule Lake.

By June 1945, the overall picture had changed. News

came of Japanese who had successfully resettled in their old towns on the West Coast. Nisei renunciants suddenly realized that their Issei parents would be leaving the camps while they themselves would be held for eventual shipment to Japan. And the war news made it obvious that Japan was beaten. Her defeat would come in a matter of weeks or, at most, months.

Now there was a move in the opposite direction—to regain the citizenship so thoughtlessly thrown away. It would take years of complex court battles and the incredible dedication of a tough San Francisco lawyer, Wayne Collins, who made their cause his own.

Collins went to Tule Lake in July and prepared form letters asking for cancellation of the applications of renunciation. By fall, the situation became graver. The government announced that the people who had given up their citizenship would be sent to Japan along with any family members who wanted to join them. With the departure time drawing near, Collins sued to force the government to halt its plans and to restore the lost U.S. citizenships.

Collins argued that renunciation of citizenship is an individual, voluntary act. The Tule Lake applications for withdrawal of citizenship were not valid, he said. They were made by people subjected to terrorist pressures from which they were not protected while under government custody. He also charged that the evacuation was unlawful and racially discriminatory. It produced conditions of unlawful pressure that led to the renunciations.

In 1949 a district court declared the renunciations invalid. But in 1950 an appeals court overturned the decision. It ruled that all of the renunciants should not have been lumped together in one case. Each case would have to be settled on an individual basis. This meant each of

In November 1945, 1500 evacuees who had given up their U.S. citizenship boarded a ship for Japan.

the renunciants had to prove that he or she withdrew citizenship because of illegal pressures. Collins filed thousands of individual applications, and the Justice Department restored citizenship on a case-by-case basis. Some of the petitions came from people who had already been sent to Japan and now wanted to return.

It took years for the applications to drag their way through the government machinery. It wasn't until 1968 that the last file was closed. All but a handful of the 5,700 renunciants were finally able to regain their citizenship. The law itself was repealed by Congress in 1947.

136

The citizenship issue affected only a small number of Japanese Americans. The overwhelming majority never thought of rejecting their country. Of greater importance to the future of the Japanese Americans was the legalized discrimination against them. The Issei were still classified as aliens not eligible to become citizens. Many West Coast states still had laws on the books preventing them from owning land or certain businesses. After the war, some states even tried to strengthen those laws.

There was a rash of land seizures in California, which confiscated Nisei-owned land on the ground that it was really owned by the Issei. California also made it illegal for Issei to hold commercial fishing licenses. Oregon, in 1945, prevented Issei from living on or using land owned by citizen relatives.

Such steps were a throwback to the racism of an earlier period. But in the postwar era, such acts were doomed. Led by the Japanese American Citizens League, the Japanese challenged these discriminatory laws in the courts and won major victories. In a series of cases, California's alien land laws were declared unconstitutional. Then the ban on Issei fishermen was also struck down by the courts. In Oregon, the state supreme court ruled its alien land law unconstitutional.

Popular opinion, once the major factor behind such laws, also changed. In 1948 California submitted a revised, much harsher alien land law to a referendum. Voters rejected it by a 3–2 margin. That signaled an end to the chapter of history in which anti-Oriental laws were the means for politicians to win support.

The final defeat of the alien land laws took years, as did the struggle to restore citizenship for renunciants. So too did settlement of the property claims of evacuees. Many had lost all their property, and all had suffered economic losses because of the evacuation and internment. In 1946 the JACL asked Congress to compensate the victims of the evacuation. In 1948 the Japanese American Evacuation Claims Act became law.

Japanese-owned property was valued at about $400 million in 1942. By 1950 about 24,000 people filed claims for losses of property amounting to about $130 million. That meant many people never claimed compensation for their wartime losses. And many of the claims that were filed were known as pots and pans cases—for small amounts to cover the loss of household goods.

The struggle for compensation became a new exercise in government discrimination. Federal investigators consistently undervalued the losses—rare bonsai trees were treated as ordinary plants, historic photos as blank film. Often the government would just reduce a claim and say "Take it or leave it." Many people took an unfair offer rather than become involved in a costly lawsuit. Others accepted unfair settlements because they were old and did not expect to live long enough to see their case go through the slow courts.

Unlike the victims of European concentration camps, not one person was compensated for loss of freedom, the death of relatives, illness, or mental suffering. Claims were paid solely on property losses, and the payments averaged about 10 percent of the true losses. Meanwhile, the government awarded over $200 million—about three-fourths of their losses—to corporations whose foreign properties had been damaged during the war.

The Japanese Americans did not get back the $400 million their property was worth in 1942 or even the $130 million total of claims filed. A mere $38 million was granted to a total of 26,500 Japanese American claimants. And even that sadly understated their true losses. The government measured their claims in terms of 1942 values. But the war had caused the value of lost homes and farms to skyrocket. The Japanese Americans were repaid in dollars worth far less than in 1942 because of inflation. It wasn't until 1965 that the last claim was finally settled.

The issue remains alive today. In 1981, Congress held hearings on the internment and, spurred by the JACL, some Congressmen backed further payments to the survivors of the camps and their heirs.

As the property claims were being considered, the JACL turned to still another major item in its agenda—removal of the laws preventing alien Japanese from becoming citizens. The Issei were unique among America's immigrants, in that they were classified as "aliens ineligible for citizenship." The campaign to change this was urgent for the Nisei. Its success would mean that their parents could become citizens in their twilight years, giving them at least partial moral compensation for their wartime sufferings.

The Immigration and Nationality Act of 1952 repealed the Oriental Exclusion Act of 1924, provided for a small annual quota of immigrants from Japan, and finally made the Issei eligible for naturalization.

Now the Issei flocked to English classes and took courses in citizenship so they could meet the requirements to become American citizens. A majority did so, including a ninety-year-old man who had been one of the first Issei to settle in America.

It took another long campaign to remove the ominous threat of future concentration camps. In 1950, Congress passed the Internal Security Act. It provided for detention of individuals simply on suspicion that they "probably will engage in, or probably will conspire with others to engage in, acts of espionage or sabotage" against the United States in an emergency. Passed during the anti-Communist hysteria of the cold war, the act was fought by civil liberties groups and by the Japanese Americans, whose experience demonstrated the abuses such a dangerous law could lead to. This "concentration camp law" was finally repealed in 1971.

Executive Order No. 9066, which authorized the evacuation, remained on the books until February 20, 1976, when President Gerald R. Ford issued a presidential proclamation revoking it. A few months later, Congress wiped away another vestige of America's wartime dishonor by repealing Public Law 503, the law which enforced the evacuation.

The legacy of the evacuation and the camps is not really measurable, but their costs are. The army spent $90 million to build and to guard the concentration camps. The WRA spent over $160 million to keep 120,000 people locked up. The inmates had done nothing to justify their imprisonment other than to be born of Japanese ancestry in a nation that was at war with Japan.

The costs to the evacuees will never be known. The $400 million estimate of property losses does not take into account the fact that land values had multiplied.

And dollar values cannot be placed on the broken hopes and shattered dreams of the Japanese American victims of the evacuation. Nor can they be applied to the flawed integrity of an entire nation that betrayed its own people.

11 The Road Back

The camps are empty now. Some have been reclaimed by the desert. The only testimony to their existence is the tombstones of the evacuees who died in them. Others still have some buildings standing—abandoned ghost towns, with wind whistling between crumbling gatehouses.

But every so often, voices are heard in the silent camps. Japanese Americans who have come to see where they and their parents had been taken, and to teach a new generation, the Sansei, about the past.

For years Japanese Americans were silent about the camps. They were a shameful memory people wanted to wipe out.

But gradually the past was faced. It could not be buried.

Crumbling barracks and gravestones—reminders that over 100,000 Japanese Americans spent most of the war years under guard

The young people were asking questions, and their Nisei parents had to confront this crucial period of their lives. As they told the Sansei of the grief that overcame the Japanese American community, of the racism that victimized them, many found relief from the knot of pain within.

Then the visits to the camps started. At first, a few families drove out; later, organized groups of several hundred people went to Tule Lake or to Manzanar. They wanted to bear witness to the past and to pay tribute to those whose lives were shattered there.

As one visitor to Manzanar said: "Some of the things I saw when I went to the Manzanar pilgrimage . . . it wasn't overt emotion, but you talk to people and they start sitting down and tears start trickling down their cheeks—that's how important the thing is. That's why it's important we look at it for sort of the mental health of the Japanese American community. You know, you have to look at these things rather than just try to bury it because it's going to come back in one form or another."

The internment was not solely a Japanese American experience. It is part of our nation's past and it tells us more about the nature of our society than many perhaps would wish to know. If memories of the period are painful for the Japanese Americans, they should also be painful for the rest of us, in whose name such terrible actions were taken.

The major reason for the evacuation was racism. America was at war with other countries in 1942, but only the Japanese were singled out for special, negative treatment. They were so chosen because of the West Coast's long history of anti-Orientalism, part of America's traditional discrimination against nonwhite people.

But even racism, by itself, would not have resulted in

the mass evacuation of the Japanese had they not been so vulnerable to attack.

Politically, they were powerless. The Issei, barred from citizenship, could not vote, and few Nisei were old enough to vote. Without the political power that comes from voting, minority groups are deprived of a key weapon of self-defense.

They were vulnerable, too, because there were so few of them. In Hawaii, where Japanese Americans formed a large portion of the population, they met with less discrimination. They were too important to the islands' economy and too entrenched in its society to be removed. On the West Coast, however, there were only a few more than 100,000 Japanese Americans. This was too small a group to properly defend itself. And it was so concentrated geographically that it could easily be dealt with.

Economically the Japanese Americans were vulnerable too. Primarily engaged in small-scale agriculture, the West Coast Japanese had no real economic power. They did not control the kinds of businesses that would make politicians court them, nor did they have the wealth that can influence others. At the same time, they did control land their neighbors wanted. Behind the patriotic rationalizations for the evacuation was the raw motive of greed: Entrenched farm interests wanted to steal the Japanese's land. The easiest way to do it was to convince the military that the Japanese had to go.

Most citizens were indifferent. They assumed that if the government said the Japanese had to be removed in the name of national security, then it should be done. There was a war on, people reasoned, and in wartime you don't take chances. Even most of those who doubted the wisdom of the action remained silent.

144

Since those days, much has changed, both for the nation and for its Japanese American citizens. Their accomplishments have gone far beyond the wildest dreams of the pre-war Japanese American community. Before the war and the camps, most were low-income farmers and workers. All were victims of discrimination.

But a generation after the camps closed, Japanese Americans had the highest median family income of any group in the country, and also the highest level of educational background. In both of these key areas, they score higher than the white majority. Over 40 percent hold high-status jobs, and about a quarter of them are professionals—a higher percentage than in any other group. Japanese Americans own about 18,000 businesses with sales of over one billion dollars annually. In 1940, only 3.8 percent were in the professions, and 25 percent worked as laborers. Crime and divorce rates among Japanese Americans are among the lowest in the country.

Once isolated and ghettoized, Japanese Americans are now assimilated into the general society. In fact, some observers fear the loss of their ethnic identity. Intermarriage with other ethnic groups is common; almost half of all Japanese American women marry outside the group. A study of the Sansei found that three-fourths had a non-Japanese among their two best friends. This is a much higher figure than among Nisei. It indicates that the Japanese Americans are among the most integrated of America's ethnic groups.

Individual Japanese Americans too have left their mark on our society. After years of political powerlessness, three U.S. senators and several congressmen of Japanese ancestry held seats in the Ninety-sixth Congress. In 1976 California, once the most anti-Japanese state in the country,

OFFICE OF SENATOR DANIEL K. INOUYE
Senator Daniel K. Inouye of Hawaii at a White House Conference

elected S. I. Hayakawa as its U.S. senator. The conservative Hayakawa even won support from the patriotic groups that once called for the removal of the Japanese.

Nisei who spent their youth in the camps have been appointed to posts as important and varied as U.S. district court judge, California state director of prisons, and similar positions. In 1974 Hawaii's George Ariyoshi became the nation's first Japanese American governor. Minoru Yamasaki and Isamu Noguchi are among the world's most famous architects and artists. Other Nisei have made significant contributions to medicine, education, science, and diplomacy.

146

Big Boy, a sculpture by the Japanese American artist Isamu
Noguchi

147

How could this happen? What made it possible for a despised minority suspected of disloyalty and confined to concentration camps to win a place in the mainstream of American life in so short a time?

Perhaps the central reason lies in the fact that after World War II, the Japanese Americans were no longer seen as a threat. Stripped of their farms and their economic resources, they were no longer competing with powerful interests on the West Coast.

California and other states had changed during the war, too. Defense industries boomed, attracting many people from states whose residents were not as prejudiced against Orientals as those on the West Coast. California's population skyrocketed. The Japanese, always a tiny proportion of the total, accounted for smaller and smaller percentages of the state's people. As racism was directed toward black and Hispanic people, discrimination against the Japanese eased somewhat.

Another factor was shame. Although most Americans supported the evacuation in a time of national danger, their mood was quite different by the war's end. Many people felt guilty about the injustice done the Japanese, especially when they learned of the magnificent combat record of the Nisei. Millions of Americans accepted their heroism as proof of the group's loyalty to the nation.

It is difficult to say which came first, the change in popular sentiment or the change in the rhetoric of political leaders. But the politicians, who did so much to stir up anti-Japanese feelings in the past, encouraged people to welcome back the returning evacuees. People tend to follow the lead of their elected officials. Just as they endorsed calls to intern the Japanese, so too were they now willing to accept Governor Warren's later calls for moderation and President Truman's praise for the Japanese Americans.

148

America's image of Japan also changed. From a war-hungry nation invading smaller and weaker countries, Japan had become a defeated nation. Two of its major cities were utterly destroyed by American atomic bombs. National shame for the use of such terrible weapons meshed with guilt over the treatment of Japanese Americans. People now felt sympathy both for Japan and for Americans of Japanese ancestry. Some years after the war, Japan bounced back from the devastation of defeat. It became an ally of the United States and one of our major trading partners.

This country changed after the war too. Postwar America was prosperous. The postwar economy boomed. Jobs and goods were plentiful, easing the pressures which lead to discrimination and opening up new opportunities. The country was also more aware of its democratic traditions after fighting a long war to preserve them. More and more people found racial discrimination distasteful.

It was also harder to stigmatize a group increasingly made up of native-born Nisei and Sansei as "strange" or "alien." The Japanese Americans were now no longer typically farmers who lived in the countryside or in small towns. After the war, almost 90 percent lived in cities. They were dispersed across the entire country, working in a variety of jobs and professions. The internment had broken traditional economic patterns. After the war, Japanese Americans entered new fields.

The camp experience also toughened the Nisei and helped them mature and develop leadership. In the camps they were part of the governing and economic structure. They exercised responsibility that would have been closed to many of them in civilian life. So they were prepared for the challenges of the postwar era.

The Nisei emerged from the camps determined to make

up for lost time and to make any necessary sacrifices. Just as the men of the 442nd put their lives on the line, so too did they and other Nisei "go for broke" to get the education needed for better jobs. They worked hard and long to prove their worth.

The Japanese Americans have become a "model minority." But despite their impressive income figures and other indicators of group success, Japanese Americans still face discrimination. Some of their fellow Americans look upon them as a people apart.

In 1975 the United States Commission on Civil Rights issued a report on the status of Asian Americans. It spotlighted numerous areas in which they remained at a disadvantage. One such area was employment. The commission found a hidden ceiling on their opportunities. Powerful corporate jobs were rarely won by Japanese Americans.

The group was largely excluded from jobs in construction, the wholesale trade, and other industries. And there was evidence that culturally biased tests and procedures, including height requirements, resulted in keeping Japanese Americans from jobs in police and fire departments.

The commission reported subtle discrimination. Elderly Issei were often forced from their homes by urban renewal programs. Such programs redeveloped neighborhoods that had had many Asian homes and businesses. Many older Asians were denied public social services to which they were legally entitled, due to language, racial and cultural barriers.

Textbooks often omitted reference to the Japanese American experience in the United States. They made no mention of the Oriental exclusion laws, the denial of citizenship rights to the Japanese, or even the fact of imprisonment in the camps during World War II. Often texts that depicted Orientals included offensive stereotypes.

Prejudice against Japanese Americans, while nowhere near past levels, still exists. A survey of Californians in the 1960s found that almost half felt the evacuation was justified—twenty-five years after it happened and after it was generally recognized there was no need for it. In 1975, a California congressman, asked about the admission of Vietnamese refugees into the country, reported that his constituents felt that, "damn it, we have too many Orientals."

Japanese Americans are still identified with Japan in ways that other ethnic Americans are not identified with their country of ancestry. When an antiwhaling group wanted to protest Japan's refusal to restrict its whaling fleet, it organized group marches in Los Angeles' Little Tokyo section and picketed local stores. Similar demonstrations would never be taken in Polish or Irish neighborhoods, for example, to protest actions by the governments of those countries.

This continuing identification with a foreign country is deeply troubling to Americans of Japanese ancestry. It means that revived persecution is possible. If America's relations with Japan were to decline, Japanese Americans might once more be discriminated against.

Recent charges that Japan was "dumping" cars, steel, and TV sets on the American market, resulting in a loss of jobs for American workers, led to a brief revival of the hated word *Jap,* and to anti-Japanese boycotts.

Japanese Americans continue to insist that, like other Americans, they be accepted as equals. They resent being subjected to racism, to stereotyping, and to identification with another country. The Japanese American Citizens

League acts as a watchdog for the community's interests. Young militants are prominent in more assertive Asian rights organizations that have sprung up in recent years.

The JACL has mounted a national reparations campaign, aimed at winning a revised financial settlement for victims of the evacuation. It has been pointed out that the evacuees got back less than a dime for every dollar lost due to the evacuation. The JACL wants those unfair economic settlements revised to take into account the violation of Japanese Americans' civil rights and their loss of liberty.

Thus, for those who were forced from their homes, the evacuation lives on as a burning issue. For others who were part of that shameful episode in American history, feelings of guilt predominate. Milton Eisenhower, the first WRA director, wrote at the time: "I feel most deeply that when the war is over . . . we as Americans are going to regret the avoidable injustices that may have been done."

One who did regret was Tom Clark, a Justice Department lawyer at the time and later a U.S. Supreme Court justice. "I have made a lot of mistakes in my life," he said publicly in 1966. "One is my part in the evacuation of the Japanese from California in 1942. . . . I don't think that served any purpose at all. . . . We picked them up and put them in concentration camps. That's the truth of the matter. And as I look back on it—although at the time I argued the case—I am amazed that the Supreme Court ever approved it."

Regret was also expressed by Earl Warren, who, as California's attorney general, was a leader in the fight for evacuation. Warren later became chief justice of the U.S. Supreme Court, and the "Warren Court" was noted for its defense of civil liberties. Throughout his life, however, he maintained silence about the evacuation. In 1974, he wrote

152

the author that the war "is now thirty years behind us, and I do not desire at this time to reconstruct it." In 1977 Warren's posthumous memoirs were published. While they say very little about his role in the evacuation, he does admit: "Whenever I thought of the innocent little children . . . I was conscience-stricken. It was wrong to act so impulsively without positive evidence of disloyalty."

Can it happen again? Will American citizens ever again be stripped of their constitutional rights and sent to concentration camps?

It would be nice to say that Americans have matured to the point at which such unconstitutional and offensive actions would never again be tolerated. But reality dictates that the possibility will be with us. America's history is marked by outbreaks of racism. In wartime especially, people tend to act on emotions more easily controlled in time of peace.

In 1943 Secretary of War Henry L. Stimson wrote: "In emergencies, where the safety of the nation is involved, consideration of the rights of individuals must be subordinated to the common security."

So long as people tolerate the idea that "the rights of individuals must be subordinated" for security's sake or for some other seemingly valid reason, outrages like the evacuation of the Japanese Americans may occur again.

Laws are no barrier; the evacuation and internment were blatantly unconstitutional. But they still took place, and the Supreme Court, in decisions that have never been revoked, approved them. In the 1950s and 1960s, laws were on the books that could have led to concentration camps for political dissenters or for persons *suspected* of disloyalty. Such laws may be passed again, and their targets may well be a racial or ethnic group.

Today, some Japanese Americans make pilgrimages to the campsites to teach their children the lessons of a bitter past.

Perhaps the best defense of our rights is to know and to remember the past, and to ensure that its mistakes are not repeated.

As one of the pilgrims to Tule Lake said: "Most of us are here today so that we can remind ourselves . . . that such things can happen in our America; that such things did happen in our America; . . . that all of us must make sure that such things do not happen again in our America."

Selected Bibliography

The following books represent only a small portion of the books, magazines, and journal articles actually consulted, but they include many readily available to the general reader. The book by Roger Daniels was the basis for interpreting the political maneuvering that led to the internment of the Japanese, although other works were helpful.

Bosworth, Allan R. *America's Concentration Camps*. New York: W. W. Norton & Co., 1967.

Conrat, Maisie and Richard. *Executive Order 9066: The Internment of 115,000 Japanese Americans*. San Francisco: California Historical Society, 1972.

Daniels, Roger. *Concentration Camps, U.S.A.: Japanese-Americans and World War II*. New York: Holt, Rinehart & Winston, 1972.

Girdner, Audrie, and Loftis, Anne. *The Great Betrayal: The Evacuation of the Japanese-Americans During World War II*. New York: Macmillan, 1969.

Hosokawa, Bill. *Nisei: The Quiet Americans*. New York: William Morrow & Co., 1969.

Houston, Jeanne Wakatsuki and James D. *Farewell to Manzanar*. Boston: Houghton Mifflin, 1973.

Inouye, Daniel K., and Elliott, Lawrence. *Journey to Washington*. Englewood Cliffs, N.J.: Prentice-Hall, 1967.

McWilliams, Carey. *Prejudice; Japanese-Americans: Symbol of Racial Intolerance*. Boston: Little, Brown & Co., 1944.

Myer, Dillon S. *Uprooted Americans: The Japanese Americans and the War Relocation Authority During World War II*. Tucson, Ariz.: University of Arizona Press, 1971.

Sone, Monica I. *Nisei Daughter*. Boston: Little, Brown & Co., 1953.

ten Broek, Jacobus; Barnhart, Edward N.; and Matson, Floyd W. *Prejudice, War and the Constitution*. Berkeley, Calif.: University of California Press, 1954.

Thomas, Dorothy Swaine. *The Salvage*. Berkeley, Calif.: University of California Press, 1952.

Thomas, Dorothy Swaine, and Nishimoto, Richard S. *The Spoilage*. Berkeley, Calif.: University of California Press, 1946.

Weglyn, Michi. *Years of Infamy: The Untold Story of America's Concentration Camps*. New York: William Morrow & Co., 1976.

Wilson, Robert A., and Hosokawa, Bill. *East to America*. New York: William Morrow & Co., 1980.

Index

Page numbers in *italics* refer to captions.

Across the Pacific, 91
American Civil Liberties
    Union, 118
American Legion, 15, 25,
    128, 131
Anti-Jap Laundry League, 15
Ariyoshi, George, 146
Arizona, 28, 44, 67
the *Arizona,* 4
Arkansas, 67
Army Intelligence Service,
    98–99
assembly centers, 46, *48, 49,*
    51–53, *51, 52,* 57–67
   education and, 63, 66

assembly centers (*continued*)
   governing of, 62–63
   Japanese American reac-
     tions to, 58–60, 61
   living conditions in, 58–
     61, *59, 60, 62,* 63–64
   Nisei vs. Issei in, 64
   security in, 51–53, *51, 52,*
     61
   work and, 58, 63–66, *65*
   see also internment camps;
     specific centers

Bainbridge Island evacuation,
    46–47
Bendetsen, Karl R., 30, 36,
    37, 44–45

158

Biddle, Francis, 9, 30, 31, 32, 35–36, 37, 115
Big Boy (Noguchi), *147*
Bill of Rights, 10
Black, Hugo, 117, 119
Blood Brothers, 81
Bogart, Humphrey, 91
Bowron, Fletcher, 131
Bronzeville, 132
Bunraku puppet shows, 73

California, 7–8, 9, 20, 28, 44, 51, 67, 132–133, 145–146
  growth of, 13, 18–19, 132, 148
  invasion fears in, 26, 27, 34
  Japanese farms in, 9
  prejudice in, 13, 16, 17, 18, 31, 33, 34, 64–65, 84, 91, 128, 130, 137, 148, 151
camouflage nets, manufacture of, 64, *65*
Camp Shelby, 103, 104
Canadian Japanese, 54
Chandler, Albert B., 91
cherry trees, Japanese, 6
Chicago, 84, 132
China, Japan's attack on, 6
Chinese Americans, 13, 32–33
Chuman, Frank, 8
Civil Control Centers, 47
Civilian Exclusion Orders, 46, 47–48
Civil War, U.S., 115
Clark, Mark, 36
Clark, Tom, 152
Collins, Wayne, 135–136
Colorado, 67

Congress, U.S., 40, 133, 136, 138, 139–140, 145
  immigration laws and, 13, 18, 139
  Tolan Committee of, 41–43
Congressional Medal of Honor, 108

Denationalization Act, 133–134
Denver, 84
De Witt, John L., 28, *28*, 29, 30, 31, 32
  evacuation administered by, 40, 44, 46, 47, 116
  evacuation sought by, 28–29, 32, 36, 37
DiMaggio, Joe, 42
discrimination, *see* racial prejudice
Distinguished Service Cross, 108, 130
Douglas, William O., 116, 117, 120

E-Day *see* Evacuation Day
Eisenhower, Milton, 45–46, 66, 152
employment, relocation and, 83–86
Endo, Mitsuye, 120, 121
Endo case, 118–121, 122, 123
enemy aliens, restrictions against, 31–32, 39, 40, 42, 44, 53, 115
Evacuation Day (E-Day), 47–49, *48*, *49*, *50*, 56–58
evacuation of Japanese Americans, 29–58, *48*, *49*, *50*, 67, 144

evacuation of Japanese Americans (*continued*)
civilian authority over, 45–46
deceptions in, 44, 45
executive order on, 37–40, *38, 39*
government calls for, 33–35, 42–43
hearings on, 41–43
Japanese American response to, 40, 41–42, 43, 48–49, *48,* 53–54, 56–57
media demands for, 32–33
military demands for, 29, 36
military force used in, 46–47, 51–53
Nisei citizenship and, 29, 33, 35–37, 41–42, 47, 53
opposition to, 9, 10, 29, 35–36, 40, 42, 115–116
public reaction to, 25, 45, 46, 54, 56, 57, 144
Executive Order No. 9066, 37–40, *38, 39,* 140

Federal Bureau of Investigation (FBI), 8, 9, 25, 29, 30, 31, 66, 80, 85, 118
Fifth Army, U.S., 104–105
Ford, Gerald R., 140
442nd Regimental Combat Team, 103–105, 106–108, 110, *111,* 130
Frankfurter, Felix, 117
Fuchida, Mitsuo, 1–2

Gentlemen's Agreement, 16
German Americans, 9

Gila internment camp, 67, 68, 89
go, 73, *74*
"Go for Broke," 103–104, 108
Goodman, Louis, 106
Granada internment camp, 67, 68
Guam, 4
Gullion, Allen, W., 30, 36, 45, 115–116

Hattiesburg, Mississippi, 104
Hawaii, 7, 11, 55, 103, 133, 144, 146
Hayakawa, S. I., 146
Heart Mountain internment camp, 67, 80, *84,* 90
Hickam Airfield, 2, 7
Hirabayashi, Gordon, 116
Hirabayashi case, 116–118, 119
Hirano, Miyuki, 57
Hollywood, *18*
Hong Kong, 4
Hood River, Oregon, 128–130
"Horizontal Hank," 108
House Committee on Un-American Activities, 91

Idaho, 28, 64, 67
Illinois, 132
immigration:
Chinese, 13
Japanese American, 11–13, 14–15, 16, 18, 20, 139
limits placed on, 11, 13, 16, 18
Immigration and Nationality Act, 139

Inouye, Daniel K., 7, 103–104, 110–112, *146*
intelligence, military, 29, 36, 98–99, 108
Internal Security Act, 139–140
internment camps:
  calls for establishment of, 25, 33, 45, 46, 54, 66, 90–91
  civilian control of, 57–58, 66, 67, 77
  cost of, 140
  death lists in, 81
  education in, 72–73, 78, 94
  government in, 72, 77, 80–81, 97
  internees' responses to, 71, *71*, 73, 77–78, 82, 90, 94
  Kibei in, 78–80, 94
  living conditions in, 68–71, *69, 70, 71,* 73
  military induction and, 87, 100–103, 106
  Nisei vs. Issei in, 72, 77, 85, 89, 90
  postwar visits to, *142,* 143, *154,* 155
  protests in, 78–82
  recreation in, 73, *74, 75, 76*
  terms for, other, 68
  views against, 45, 66, 83–84, 115–116
  work in, 72–73, 78
  see also specific camps
Issei, 20–22, 23, 24
  careers of, 13–14, 15, 16–17, 18–19, *19,* 20, 21

Issei (*continued*)
  goals and values of, 13, 16, 17, 20–21, 22, 56
  Nisei internees in conflict with, 72, 77, 85, 89, 90
  postwar citizenship of, 139
  protests led by, 80–82
Italian Americans, 9

Jackson, Robert H., 119
Japan, 11, *12,* 149, 151
  declaration of war against, 6
  Japanese Americans and, 15–16, 17, 21, 23, 24, 31, 97, 122, *136,* 151
  Pearl Harbor attacked by, 1–6, *3, 5,* 7
Japanese American Citizens League (JACL), 9, 24–25, 37, 44, 80–81, 92
  evacuation accepted by, 40, 53–54, 80
  military recruitment favored by, 100, 106
  postwar activities of, 137, 138, 139, 151–152
Japanese American Evacuation Claims Act, 138
Japanese American military units, 78, 85–86, 87, 98–112, *105, 111,* 124, 128, 130–131
  combat record of, 104, 105, 107–109, 130–131
  intelligence work of, 98–99, 108
  loyalty oaths for, 87, 102, 106
  military treatment of, 98, 101, 104–105, 108–109

Japanese American military
units (*continued*)
Occupation forces in Japan, service with, 99
recruitment of, 100–103
see also 442nd Regimental
Combat Team; 100th
Infantry Battalion
Japanese Americans:
camps revisited by, *142,*
143
leadership among, 20,
53–54, 149
Nisei vs. Issei among, 8,
17, 20, 21–22, 23, 24,
29, 33, 41, 42, 72, 77,
85, 89, 90
postwar discrimination
against, 126, 128–130,
137, 148–149, 150–152
postwar role of, 145–152
prewar discrimination
against, 7, 13, 14–18,
18, 22, 23, 24, 143–144
rumors about, 6, 15, 24,
26–27, 31
Japanese Imperial Navy, 2,
27
Jerome internment camp, 67,
69, *70,* 124, *125*
Journey to Washington (Inouye), 110
Justice Department, U.S., 29,
30, 32, 37, 115, 133–
134, 136

Kabuki drama, 73, *75*
Kansas, 45
kenjinkai, 21
Kenney, Robert W., 131

Kibei, 78–80, 94, 109
legal position of, 115
loyalty oaths and, 89
Knox, Frank, 26
Korean Americans, 32–33
Korematsu, Fred, 118, 119
Korematsu case, 118–120,
122
Kozasa, Betty, 61
Kurihara, Joe, 81–82
Kuroki, Ben, 109

Latin American Japanese, 54–
55
Life magazine, 24
Little Tokyo, 14, 132, 151
Los Angeles, 14, 20, 31, 43,
50, 129, 131, 132, 151
"Los Angeles, Battle of," 43
Los Angeles *Examiner,* 97
"Lost Battalion," 107, 108
loyalty oaths, 83–84, 86–90
camp uprisings caused by,
89, 90
family disruption caused
by, 89, 90
for Nisei in service, 87,
102, 106

McCloy, John J., 36, 99–100
McLemore, Henry, 33
Malaya, 4
Manzanar Assembly Center,
45, *49, 52,* 58, *59,* 64
Manzanar *Free Press,* 63
Manzanar internment camp,
67, 68, *69,* 80–81, 89,
143
Marshall, George C., 122
Masaoka, Mike, 41–42, 100,
109, 110

Merrill's Marauders, 108
Midway Island, 4
Military Area Number One, 44, 46
Military Area Number Two, 44
Milligan case, 115, 119
Minidoka internment camp, 67, 68, 89, 102–103
Montana, 28, 44, 64
Murata, Hideo, 57
Murphy, Frank, 117, 119–120, 121
Myer, Dillon, 83, *84,* 95, 120

Nakada family, 109
National Conference of Governors (1943), 91
National Origins Act, 18
New York City, 7
Nippon Patriotic Society, 96
Nisei:
 Americanism of, 19, 22, 23, 24–25, 37, 77–78
 citizenship rights of, 29, 33, 35–37, 41–42, 47, 53, 115, 116–123, 135–137, 139
 draft status of, 78, 98, 105–107
 education of, 16, 22–23, *34,* 150
 goals and values of, 21–22, 23, 24–25, 149–150
 Issei internees in conflict with, 72, 77, 85, 89, 90
 military role of, *see* Japanese American military units
 prewar careers of, 16, 23

Noguchi, Isamu, 146, *147*

Office of War Information (OWI), 99
the *Oklahoma,* 3–4
100th Infantry Battalion, 103, 104, *105,* 106–107
Oregon, 28, 44, 64, 130, 137
Oriental Exclusion Act, 139

Pacific Fleet, U.S., 2, 4, 26
Pearl Harbor, attack on, 1–6, *3, 5, 7*
 American reaction to, 4, 5, 6–8, 26–27, 29
 Japanese Americans and, 6–10, 55, 98
 losses suffered in, 4, 26
Perry, Matthew C., 11
Philippine Islands, 4, 31, 99
Poston Assembly Center, 45
Poston internment camp, 67, 68, 72, 77, 79–80, 126, *127*
Potato King, The, 19
Pratt, Henry C., 123
Presidential Unit Citation, 108, 110
Public Law 503, 40, 140
Purple Heart, 107
Puyallup Assembly Center, 46, 58, 61

Quakers, 66, 85

racial prejudice, 32–33, 143
 in California, 13, 16, 17, 18, 31, 33, 34, 64–65, 84, 91, 128, 130, 137, 148, 151

racial prejudice (*continued*)
    economic motives for, 13,
        14, 15, 33, 144, 149,
        151
    immigration laws and, 11,
        13, 16, 17–18
    Pearl Harbor and, 6, 7, 8–
        10
    politics and, 15, 137, 144
    repudiations of, official,
        9–10, 100, *101*, 109,
        131, 132
    in South, 104
    unions and, 15, 130
    war as spur to, 7, 10, 32,
        153
    see also Japanese Ameri-
        cans
raids, FBI, 8, 29, 30–31,
    43–44
Red Cross, 9
release from internment, Ja-
    panese American, 121–
    136, *125, 127, 129,* 137
    Issei vs. Nisei in, 124, 126,
        134, 135
    Japanese American re-
        sponses to, 124, 126,
        128, 132
    public reaction to, 128–
        132, 148
    renunciation of citizenship
        and, 133–137, *136*
    Supreme Court and, 120–
        122
    WRA and, 121, 123, 126,
        128
relocation centers, *see* in-
    ternment camps
relocation, internee, 83–86,
    86, 87, 92, 120, 124

Roberts, Owen, 117, 121
Rohwer internment camp, 67,
    69, *86*
Roosevelt, Franklin D.:
    declaration of war by, 6
    discrimination repudiated
        by, 9–10, 100
    Japanese American intern-
        ment and, 66, 68
    Japanese American release
        and, 122
    Japanese evacuation and,
        9–10, 36–37, *38,* 45
Roosevelt, Theodore, 16

Salt Lake City, 84, 126
San Francisco, 14, 16, 31,
    130–131
    Chronicle, 14
    earthquake, 16
Sansei, 141, 143, 145
Santa Anita Assembly Cen-
    ter, 51, *51, 52,* 60–61,
    62, 64, 79
Santa Barbara, 43
Seattle, 14
Shima, George, 19
Silver Star, 108
Singapore, 4
Sone, Monica, 56, 58, 68
South, racial segregation in,
    104
South Dakota, 44
Stanford University, 15
stereotypes, Japanese Ameri-
    can, 15, 22
Stilwell, Joseph (Vinegar
    Joe), 130–131
Stimson, Henry L., 32, 36–
    37, *39,* 45, 122, 153

Supreme Court, U.S., 34,
115, 116–123, 153

Taft, Robert A., 40
Tajiri, Larry, 7
Tanaka, Togo, 88
Tanforan Assembly Center,
58–59, *60*
Terminal Island evacuation,
43–44
Texas, 108
Thailand, 4
Tolan, John H., 41
Tolan Committee, 41–43
Topaz internment camp, 67,
68, 79, 89
Truman, Harry S., 106, 110,
148
Tule Lake internment camp,
67, 68–69, 72, 92–94,
93, 114, 120, 155
Tule Lake Segregation Cen-
ter, 92–97, *93,* 126,
133–135

United Nations Conference
(San Francisco), 131–
132
United States:
invasion rumors in, 6, 26,
27, 43
security measures in, 8–
10, 29, 31–32, 39,
139–140
United States Commission on
Civil Rights, 150
Uno, Ernest, 110
Utah, 28, 64, 67

Vietnamese refugees, 151

Vosges mountains, battle of,
107

Wakatsuki, Jeanne, 58
Wake Island, 4
War Department, U.S., 29,
31, 36–37, 38, 40,
105–106, 109, 122
civilian conflicts with, 29–
30, 32, 37
War Relocation Authority
(WRA), 45–46, 57–58,
66, 67, 68, 72, 73, 77,
121, 140
closing of camps by, 123,
126, 128
military recruitment and,
99, 106
relocation plans favored
by, 66, 83–84, 85, 87,
92, 120, 121
Tule Lake Segregation Center and, 92, 95, 97
Warren, Earl, 34–35, *35,*
42–43, 91, 131, 148,
152–153
"Warren Court," 152
Wartime Civil Control Ad-
ministration (WCCA),
44–45, 47
Washington, D.C., 6
Washington, state of, 28, 44,
130
Western Defense Command,
28, 123
the *West Virginia,* 4
Wheeler Field, 2, *5*
Wilson, Woodrow, 17
World War II:
American entry into, 2,
4–6

World War II (*continued*)
    European Theater of, 5,
      104–105, 107
    Japanese expansion in, 4, 6
WRA, *see* War Relocation
    Authority

Wyoming, 64, 67

Yamasaki, Minoru, 146
Yasui, Kenny, 109
Yellow Peril, The, 15

166

940.5472 Davis, Daniel S.
DAV
          Behind barbed
          wire

    $15.95   10453